"I'll just go take a shower while you order a peperoni pizza."

Cameron trapped Halina neatly between his arms. "There are two things wrong with your suggestion."

"Really?" she said.

"First, I like mushrooms on my pizza and second," he pushed his body gently against her, "*you* won't be taking a shower. *We* will."

Halina's breathing quickened. "I thought you were going to tell me about your car accident."

"All in good time," he told her, nuzzling her neck.

"But *I* want information." She tried to evade his seeking mouth, but it unerringly found a sensitive target.

"And *I*," Cameron said huskily, "want *you!*"

Dear Reader:

As the months go by, we continue to receive word from you that SECOND CHANCE AT LOVE romances are providing you with the kind of romantic entertainment you're looking for. In your letters you've voiced enthusiastic support for SECOND CHANCE AT LOVE, you've shared your thoughts on how personally meaningful the books are, and you've suggested ideas and changes for future books. Although we can't always reply to your letters as quickly as we'd like, please be assured that we appreciate your comments. Your thoughts are all-important to us!

We're glad many of you have come to associate SECOND CHANCE AT LOVE books with our butterfly trademark. We think the butterfly is a perfect symbol of the reaffirmation of life and thrilling new love that SECOND CHANCE AT LOVE heroines and heroes find together in each story. We hope you keep asking for the "butterfly books," and that, when you buy one—whether by a favorite author or a talented new writer—you're sure of a good read. You can trust all SECOND CHANCE AT LOVE books to live up to the high standards of romantic fiction you've come to expect.

So happy reading, and keep your letters coming!

With warm wishes,

Ellen Edwards

Ellen Edwards
SECOND CHANCE AT LOVE
The Berkley/Jove Publishing Group
200 Madison Avenue
New York, NY 10016

SWEET ABANDON
DIANA MARS

SECOND CHANCE AT LOVE
BOOK

To my parents

Chapter

1

HALINA BARKLEY ALMOST dropped the delicate creamer of the demitasse service when a loud, peremptory knock sounded on her door. She carefully placed the gold Mocha piece she'd been cleaning on the inlaid pedestal table by the window and, rubbing her hands on the worn bib apron that covered her gray skirt and blouse, walked quickly out of the dining room. She was surprised that any of her tenants might be requiring her services, since they had all said everything was running smoothly when she had collected the rent checks the day before.

She opened the door with a ready smile, brushing away a strand of chestnut hair that had come undone from her ponytail. Her smile froze and her gray eyes widened as she saw who stood outside her door. Halina had to look up a considerable distance to reach the light-green eyes that were regarding her with a mixture of appreciation and amusement. The raven-haired man was at least a foot taller than her own five-five, and the wide-as-a-barn shoulders belonged on a football player. Her eyes continued their curious perusal and slowly descended the long, muscular length of the stranger, taking in the expertly tailored forest-green suit, silk shirt opened at the neck, and handmade suede-and-leather shoes. The broad shoulders, flat stomach, and long legs snugly encased in the expensive suit radiated pure sexual energy, and when a grin uncovered a set of even white teeth, Halina steeled her body to resist the overwhelming magnetism of the man.

Her dazed eyes registered movement of the man's sensually molded lips, and she realized belatedly he must be saying something. Forcing her wandering mind to concentrate, she picked up on the last words the man was uttering.

". . . see the manager, H. Barkley."

After long years of practice, Halina quickly regained her composure, and, unconsciously straightening, she said coolly, "I'm Halina Barkley, the manager. How may I help you?"

Halina glimpsed the surprise in the man's pale eyes before it was swiftly veiled by the thick black lashes. She had to hide a smile at the thought that they were now even: Her surprise at seeing such a perfect specimen of manhood had been equaled by his own finding that she was the manager. She had purposely concealed her identity in newspaper advertisements, and the sign outside her door simply said, in small capital letters, H. BARKLEY—MANAGER. Since her father's name had been Hal, and Halina had continued to sign all checks "H. Barkley," not many people other than her tenants and lawyer knew that Halina had taken over the administration of the building after her father's death a year ago.

The man looked her up and down again, as if trying to fit this new piece of information into his previous assessment. Halina sustained his deliberate scrutiny with equanimity, knowing she appeared a few years younger than her actual twenty-seven. With her peaches-and-cream complexion tinged a healthy pink from the exertions of spring cleaning and her long chestnut hair rebelling against the constraining rubber band, spilling gleaming strands about her rounded face, she looked more like a teenager.

Waiting for the stranger to speak, Halina eyed him speculatively. His hesitation was quite out of keeping with the aura of command and power he exuded, and Halina guessed he did not have to reconsider first impressions often. But all signs of uncertainty disappeared as he said briskly, "I saw your ad in the paper, but there was no Apartment for Rent sign outside. Has it been taken yet?"

Halina blinked. Although her building was fairly modern, built in an inverted U shape surrounding a flower-filled courtyard and a small fountain, she couldn't believe that a man like him would be looking for an apartment in her area.

A new thought occurred to her—perhaps the man was looking at the apartment for a friend or relative. She answered him automatically, "I never post signs outside I deal only through newspaper ads—and local ones at that." She was about to add that crackpots were more easily avoided that way when he interrupted her with mocking condescension.

"Do you think we might finish conducting our conversation somewhere other than the hallway?"

Aware that she would have invited him inside long ago if he had been someone else, Halina swallowed the cutting remark that rose to her lips. The man obviously mistook her reticence, for he said softly, "I can assure you I am not a practicing rapist. I haven't ravished a young maiden in many a full moon."

Halina hid the smile that tugged at her full red lips and motioned him in, noticing that the man left the door ajar. She walked quickly into the study, which she had barely changed since her father's death. She had only replaced the faded curtains with new gold-and-rust-striped floor-length ones, which matched the rust of the thick carpeting and the gold velour of a large hideaway couch she used when preparing or correcting finals for the two courses she taught, European civilization and history of science.

She indicated one of the two tobacco armchairs as she went around the impressive walnut desk. The man waited politely until she was seated in the leather swivel chair before he folded his own imposing bulk into the comfortable chair directly facing her.

Halina waited for him to speak, but when he just sat there lazily regarding her with his disturbing green eyes, she decided she had used enough time from her busy schedule.

"Now, then," she began in her crisp professional voice, "how may I help you, Mr. . . . ?"

"Connors, Cameron Connors," he supplied smoothly. "Cam to my friends."

"Mr. Connors," she emphasized subtly. "This is getting repetitious, but is there something I can do for you?" Halina allowed some of her impatience to show in her voice. It appeared this man was used to women waiting for every word to drop like gold from his sexy firm lips.

"You *could* do a lot for me, Miss Barkley," he said in a low, suggestive tone, his devastating smile deepening the carved laugh lines on lean cheeks, turning his eyes a feral green. "Unfortunately, at the moment I'm pressed for time. I really came to inquire about the apartment." Checking his ultrathin gold watch, he added, "I'm running late already. I have a five o'clock appointment."

How typical of a man! Her time was just as important, as much at a premium, as his. "As a matter of fact, Mr. Connors, *you* are interrupting my schedule. I have a class in less than three hours and I have yet to finish preparing a lesson. As for my doing anything for you of a sexual nature," she continued in a low dulcet tone, "which is what you implied with your innuendo. Aren't you taking a lot for granted? Including the fact that even if I did succumb to your dubious charm, I certainly would not be at the disposal of your busy schedule?"

Halina saw a look of surprise leap into his eyes and was thrilled that she had completely disconcerted him.

He in turn surprised her by apologizing. "You're right. I'm sorry. I *am* taking a lot for granted." Grinning audaciously, he added huskily, "But that's because you don't know me very well. You'll see, I'll grow on you quickly."

"Like cancer, no doubt."

"Like a carefully aged wine," he retorted promptly, and then suddenly sat back in the chair. Halina eyed him with concern as he took a pristine handkerchief from his back pocket and wiped his forehead and mouth. He appeared to be ill, but before she could speak, he rallied and said in a soft, seductive tone, "I just thought we could bypass some of the usual games."

Halina raised one finely arched brow. "Games? I guess I'd better make it clear from the outset—I don't come with the building."

"Pity," he said with an infuriatingly confident smile. "You do wonders for the value of the neighborhood."

"There's nothing wrong with this neighborhood," she was quick to point out. "It's a fine, handsome community, with lots of services and a terrific location, close to the lake and yet near enough to the Loop to make it practical as well as appealing."

"You sound enamored of it—and of your building," he teased gently.

"Not enamored—just proud of both," she answered matter-of-factly. "I know that you're probably more at home in surroundings like the Gold Coast or Marina City—"

"You shouldn't judge a book by its cover," he told her softly.

"Likewise, I'm sure." She hated the amusement she saw glittering in his pond-colored eyes. But she really couldn't blame him. "You said something about an apartment Mr. Connors?" she asked calmly.

"Yes, I would like to rent an apartment for three or four months."

Halina's eyes narrowed, and she studied him over the steeple her hands had formed across her pursed mouth.

"I believe it was made quite clear in the ad that the apartment was to be rented only on a year lease."

He passed a hand through his hair impatiently, ruffling its organized riotousness even more. "I realize that. I've tried to find a decent place to rent since I came in from Texas last week, but most seem to require a year's lease." Her eyebrows went up at that, and he added by way of explanation, "I need a place that's centrally located, close to stores and public transportation and the lake—which you've already indicated Barkley Court is. In short, I must have a place where I would not need a car, and it must be spacious enough for my requirements." He gestured at their surroundings and added, "From the look of this apartment, it seems I've found exactly what I need."

Halina caught herself wondering what Cameron Connors's requirements might be—another sign that the man had affected her tranquillity and general indifference toward men—but it was not enough to make her continue a conversation that would lead nowhere.

"I'm sorry, Mr. Connors," she said, rising from her chair to indicate that their talk was concluded, "but my rule is one-year leases. If you would care to leave your number, perhaps I can find something else for you."

Cameron Connors stood, raising a detaining hand. "No, please." The word "please" came out somewhat strangled, as if he had never used it before. "I could make it worth your while."

Halina took a deep breath and exhaled slowly. The man did not give up. "Mr. Connors, I'm afraid I can't make an exception. I've turned down other people who requested less than a year's lease."

"All right. I'll pay you for the whole year," he cut in swiftly.

Halina looked at him, nonplussed. "But there are real estate agencies out there, Mr. Connors, who could probably find you . . ."

"You're not much of a businesswoman, Halina Barkley, if you can let a good deal like this pass," he said with a smile that contained some of the potency he'd displayed. But with the afternoon sun flooding through the open-curtained window, Halina remembered her earlier thought that he might be ill. The pallor of Cameron Connors's face and the dark shadows ringing his eyes beneath the deep tan told her that whatever ailed him was more than just the flu. And she found herself reconsidering turning him away.

"All right," she said at length. "If you're willing to pay triple for a four-month stay, it's your loss, my gain. I'll contact my lawyer and he can set up a modified lease with new provisions. But you know that for the kind of money you're prepared to pay, you could easily get a room at a major hotel, and you wouldn't have to clean or cook for yourself."

His pleasantly deep chuckle chased chills up and down her spine. "Honest till the end, aren't you, Halina Barkley? You'd be surprised to know how often I've fended for myself, and I actually enjoy cooking. So don't worry, I know exactly what I'm doing." He fixed her with a discomfiting stare. "I was just thinking, though, that perhaps I might need six months after all."

Halina sighed. She had never acted on impulse—certainly not out of kindness to the male sex, except for her father. Now he was considering extending his stay. Of course, she could always renege; nothing had been signed yet. But for reasons she didn't care to dwell on at the moment, she knew she'd not go back on her word.

"The price agreed on is more than sufficient, Mr. Connors. Would you care to see the apartment now?"

He looked at his watch again and shook his head. "I assume its dimensions are basically the same as this one?"

Halina nodded. "Yes, although the distribution of the rooms is reversed. Are you sure you don't want to see it before taking it?"

"No, I know all I need to. I'm running late already."

Halina came around from behind her desk to show him out, suddenly realizing that their encounter had left her strangely exhausted. It came as a surprise, since she slept well and was in good shape, playing tennis and swimming daily at the nearby YMCA.

Although he'd mentioned having an appointment, he didn't seem in any rush to leave, and Halina wanted him out as soon as possible. The fact that he was capable of draining her made her uncomfortable. She asked him briskly, "When were you planning on moving in?"

"Tomorrow."

Though startled, Halina maintained her lack of expression. She extended her hand to seal their agreement. "I'll have my lawyer prepare the new lease tonight."

"No need to rush, Miss Barkley. I'll leave you the first month's rent and a security deposit." At her nod he counted out the bills and handed them to her.

Halina retraced her steps around the desk and took a receipt book from the top drawer. After writing the amount and signing with crisp efficiency, she gave him the receipt, which he stuffed in his wallet. Then he placed the wallet in his pocket.

The movement opened the dark-green jacket and strained the buttons on his shirt, so that for a moment his muscles were well delineated underneath the thin material, revealing the thick mat of hair covering his chest in a dark tapering triangle just as clearly. What held Halina's attention was the raw red scar just barely visible above the top button of his shirt. It was at least two inches wide, and Halina was sure it extended quite a length. As he straightened again, he automatically closed his jacket, and looked up to find her eyes on him. Halina held her breath, her stomach turning over from the sight of the ugly wound. His eyes held hers, but Halina neither blushed nor lowered her own gaze. She noticed again the whiteness underneath the tan, and now that she was closer to him, she could see the tiny drops of perspiration dotting his wide forehead and surrounding the firm lips.

It was Cameron Connors who finally looked away. He pivoted sharply and left the study with long strides. As she followed him at a slower pace, Halina knew that something in her own eyes had stripped away his easy charm and left raw emotion in its wake.

But when he turned at the door, his features were impassive. He extended his hand and Halina shook it, noticing how her small palm was swallowed by the bronzed largeness of his.

"I hope Barkley Court does satisfy all your needs, Mr. Connors," she said, withdrawing her hand from his and from the titillating touch of his thumb caressing her palm with expert eroticism.

An expression she couldn't decipher crossed Cameron Connors's face. When he spoke again, he sounded like the man she'd opened the door to only half an hour before.

"Oh, I think it will, Halina Barkley," he drawled before turning one final time and striding down the thickly carpeted corridor.

Chapter

2

"HELLO, MR. QUE," Halina greeted the fiftyish man brightly as she juggled her purse and a grocery bag in one arm, and another large grocery bag in the other.

Randolph Que quickly stood up, laying his gardening tools on the ground and wiping his muddied hands on his overalls. "Here, let me take this bag," he said as he helped Halina with her purchases.

"No, that's all right," Halina protested, but relinquished her hold gracefully when a tug-of-war developed. Leading the way into the building, she held the front door open for her favorite tenant. "How are the tomatoes coming along?"

"Terrific," he exclaimed. "And I think I'll be able to check on your strawberries before I go downtown tonight."

Halina shook her head as she unlocked the door to her apartment. "You already do too much for me, Mr. Que. Giving me free judo lessons, helping with the garden and around the house..."

"Please," he interrupted her as he set down the groceries on the oval kitchen table and raised a powerful blunt-fingered hand. "I will always be grateful for the emotional *and* financial support I received from your dad when Hal let Sylvia and I stay on without paying rent for five months." His brown eyes glazed over with the sadness that had not been erased in four years, since his wife had finally succumbed to cancer.

"But, Mr. Que," Halina said, tears burning the backs

of her eyes at the sight of the kindly man's grief, which seldom surfaced, "you already repaid my father—and me, especially—with all your kindnesses."

"It's my pleasure." He put his hand on her shoulder in one of his rare gestures of affection, silencing her words of gratitude. "You know how my wife and I had wanted children...we always looked upon you as a daughter."

The tears threatened to break through, but Halina blinked them back determinedly. She had always prided herself on her self-control and knew Randolph Que would be embarrassed by overt emotion. Nonetheless, she took his hand in both of hers and squeezed it tightly for one brief moment before emptying the grocery bags and transferring the perishable items to the refrigerator with brisk concentration.

"May I offer you some refreshment?" she asked when she was certain her voice would not betray her.

"No, thank you." His voice was gruff with emotion, and he cleared his throat before he spoke again. "I'd like to get back to the tomatoes, and then I'd better clean up. I think a good bath is in order," he added in a more normal tone, looking down at his dirt-plastered overalls.

Halina laughed, glad to break the tension, and told him that he did indeed look disreputable.

Randolph Que smiled and asked her, "Will you be able to make practice on Tuesday?"

Halina nodded vigorously. "And you can guess what kind of cookies I'll bring." Ever since Randolph Que had started giving her martial-arts lessons a few months ago, she had sought some way to repay him, since he refused to charge her for private sessions, which usually commanded a high price. Halina had discovered recently that not only was he an expert in his field, but he also possessed an incurable sweet tooth, which was, amazingly, not reflected in his impeccably white teeth nor in his weight. So each time she had a lesson, Halina gave him something she had baked and teased him about his good fortune.

As Halina saw him out, he commented casually, "By the way, your new tenant, the one who moved in last week, Mr. . . . ."

"Connors," Halina supplied with a quizzical look, knowing Randolph Que seldom spoke of the other tenants and, unless sought out, kept mostly to himself.

"Yes, that's it. Mr. Connors." His shrewd dark eyes rested on her face. "He seems quite a nice young man."

Nice young man? Halina almost laughed out loud. But she saw the seriousness of Randolph Que's gaze, and sobered.

"I really haven't seen much of him," she began cautiously.

"Oh, I have a feeling you will," Randolph Que said matter-of-factly.

Halina blinked, not knowing what to make of the unusual twinkle in the kind brown eyes or of his cryptic statement. Flustered, she said, "I—I imagine I will. He'll be giving me his check monthly, and I suppose he might need other things in between . . ." But Randolph Que was already letting himself out, stopping long enough to add a quiet bombshell.

"He expressed intense admiration for you. He told me he was quite surprised to see that you manage the building so well, doing a lot of work you could just as well hire others to do."

No doubt, Halina thought cynically. That is probably what *he* would do. She had already seen the careless way he carried money, and his commanding, confident manner spoke of his wealth. He could easily afford to pay other people, just as easily as he paid the rent.

"You know that throwing myself into all kinds of activities was a form of therapy after my father's death. It brought home the fact that I had to rely on myself, since I had no other living relatives."

"I know you *always* liked to keep busy. Your father once said you were a workaholic." As he climbed the stairs, he added a final parting shot: "Your Mr. Connors said it was refreshing to see a person who actually enjoys working."

Halina stood staring at the back of his graying head, unable to declare that Mr. Connors was not, nor ever would be, hers.

Ruefully shaking her head, she closed the door and headed for the bedroom to change into her tennis outfit. She had agreed to play Ted Lander, whom she'd met at the club where they both held memberships. They had been dating for the past few weeks, ever since he'd suggested they go out to celebrate after a terrific doubles win. She'd have to hurry. Ted was a very impatient man.

Forty minutes later, after shelving the rest of her groceries and taking a quick shower, Halina was dressed in a yellow top and a brief white skirt. She took one last look in the full-length mirror covering the bathroom door, noticing the way the tiny pleats of the new skirt barely reached the top curves of her long, slender thighs and outlined her generous hips.

She had always tended toward plumpness, and her worst fear in adolescence had been that her baby fat would become permanent. But her reflection put to rest her old childhood doubts. Although she had never grown the extra inches she'd prayed for, her baby fat had distributed itself nicely, with a definite concentration on her bustline and hips and a total absence of it in the firm buttocks, tiny waist, and shapely legs.

Halina picked up her tennis bag, impatiently brushing away the chestnut strands that fell against her cheeks when she stooped.

As she stepped out of her apartment, she perceived a

movement and automatically looked to her left. Cameron Connors was staring at her, his arm arrested in the act of opening his own door. Halina couldn't see his eyes clearly at that distance, but he had an air of stillness and intensity that made her feel unaccountably uncertain.

The spell was broken as he pocketed his keys and walked toward her. Halina was irritated by the way his gaze traveled deliberately over her, from her sneakered feet to her gold-ribboned hair. The mocking light in his eyes acknowledged her displeasure, but it certainly did not faze him.

After her disastrous experience with Jeff—and a later, equally unsatisfying relationship—Halina had woven an impregnable net about herself. She only dated men she knew posed no emotional danger for her. Cameron Connors was definitely not in that category.

"Something else we have in common," he drawled lazily, indicating her tennis gear.

"I didn't realize we knew each other well enough to have anything in common, Mr. Connors," she retorted coolly. As she locked her door, Halina thought she heard him mutter what sounded suspiciously like, "Something I intend to remedy."

When she gave him a sharp look, his light-green eyes were limpid as a baby's. But behind the blandness of his gaze she saw the light of challenge, which she wasn't about to acknowledge or accept. She was already running late, and Ted. . . . Goodness, Ted! He was bound to be furious. She had begged off the last two dinner dates, and he would not be pleased if she showed up late today. He would be anxious to begin. Although Halina liked tennis, she did not have Ted's fierce competitive spirit and did not play solely to win. Unfortunately for Ted's rather fragile ego, though, she had won the last three games, and he was itching for a rematch.

Cameron Connor's voice cut through her musings like a finely honed blade.

"Need a partner?"

Halina clutched her bag convulsively. His words had taken on a seductive quality and she had the feeling that his opening gambit was undoubtedly used with great frequency and high results. What bothered her was the fact that someone like Cam Connors could affect her when she had been successfully fighting off wolves for years.

Forcing herself to look him straight in the eye, Halina answered calmly, "No, thank you. I already have one."

"Perhaps another time," he said smoothly.

Looking over her shoulder, she gave him a saccharine smile and said just as sweetly, "Perhaps."

Her quick glance had revealed that he'd made no move to enter his apartment. He still stood in the hallway, his hands stuffed in his pockets, stretching the beige material of his slacks, his dark brown sport coat opened to reveal the intimidating powerful chest. She found herself visualizing him in a tight tennis outfit and made a lightning-swift comparison of his physique with Ted Lander's. The direction of her thoughts appalled her and her shoulders stiffened, as much in rejection of the images as in instinctive response to the eyes she felt scorching into her back until she disappeared from view with an audible sigh of relief.

Halina turned on the oven to heat the chicken and fries she'd picked up on the way home and plopped down in the wicker chair with a groan. The ringing of the phone elicited a louder groan, and she dragged her bare feet across the cool parquet floor to answer it. She leaned on the green-and-white wall as she picked up the receiver, and said with less than her usual cordiality, "Barkley residence."

There was a chuckle on the other end, its velvety richness unmistakable. Just the sound of it put some starch in Halina's sagging back, and his words restored almost all of the adrenaline lost in her epic struggle with Ted.

"I'm sure glad I'm not at death's door, because I have a feeling I'd receive no help or compassion from you tonight. What happened? Lose all your games?"

"Not that it's any of your business, but no. I won almost every game," she shot back.

"So how come you took so long to get home?"

His audacity silenced Halina, but not for long. "Would you get to the point, Mr. Connors?" In the morning she would worry about having been abrupt with a tenant, but at the moment she was too incensed and exhausted to care about amenities.

"My, my. Totally out of sorts, aren't we?" he goaded. Halina bit her lip to prevent herself from rising to the bait, telling herself that coolness was her best defense against this insufferable man.

"What may I do for you, Mr. Connors?" she asked in a voice that reflected only a weary patience rather than the volcano brewing inside her, which was ready to explode from Ted's childishness and Cameron Connors's taunting.

His rich laugh sent a tingle along her skin. She knew what was going through his mind, and although she should have found his suggestive laugh insulting, she was not offended. And that infuriated her even more.

"Look, Mr. Connors. I'm tired, I'd like to take a bath, and I have a counseling session tomorrow morning, which I consider far more important than our chitchat." She added silkily, "Pleasant though it may be."

"Well, then, I'll come straight to the point." His officious tone mocked her with its undercurrent of amusement. "The light on the back porch is burned out, and I'd appreciate it if you'd come over and fix it."

Halina looked disgustedly at the mushroom-shaped clock. "Mr. Connors, it's almost ten o'clock. I'll get to it tomorrow."

"It'll only take a few seconds, Miss Barkley."

"Then why don't you replace it yourself?" she said with feigned sweetness.

"If I'd had spare bulbs in the apartment, I would have. But they seem in short supply at the moment," he countered smoothly.

Halina breathed deeply. "All right, Mr. Connors. I'll be right there!" She hung up the phone with a crash that almost brought it down from its wall fixture, and opened the door of the pantry, where bulbs were stacked neatly on two shelves. She picked up a large opaque one and slammed the door shut. Turning off the oven, from which a mouth-watering smell emanated, she wished an unpleasant destination for Cameron Connors. Grabbing the keys from the pedestal table on the way out, she marched down to his apartment in a rage.

Halina banged on the door twice, her knuckles helping to vent her anger. As soon as it opened, she thrust the bulb into Cameron Connors's hand. Turning swiftly, she began striding away, only to be pulled up short by a firm grip on her arm.

"Hey, not so fast," he said as he swung her around. He held the bulb with the other hand, grinning. "Aren't you going to put it in?"

"Do you know, Mr. Connors, what you can do with that damn light bulb?" Halina choked out, her breath coming in short rasps, as if she'd just run a marathon.

He let go of her and, crossing his arms, arched one mocking brow. "No, tell me. I might learn something."

Halina opened her mouth, but no sound came out. She was speechless. Knowing the picture she must make, gaping like a fish, while he stood there with that superior look on his handsomely carved features, she grabbed the bulb and stalked into his apartment. He followed her with deceptive laziness, and leaned negligently against the doorjamb while she stood on tiptoe and stretched her body to the fullest, silently cursing him and her lack of inches in equal measure but too tired to argue any further.

"You are really engaging in reverse discrimination," he remarked casually. "Had I been a woman, you would have replaced it with far more grace and diligence."

Halina glared back at him over her shoulder but said nothing as she began screwing in the new bulb with barely controlled violence. The tired muscles of her calf cramped and she felt her balance shifting. Trying to save the bulb, she instinctively placed more weight on her numb calf, and her legs buckled. The next instant, as visions of herself falling in an ignominious heap at his feet flashed through her mind, Cameron Connors's arm circled her waist and his hard warm body easily absorbed Halina's weight.

She noticed dazedly that the bulb had also been saved. Cameron leaned forward and, protectively tightening his grip on her slender waist, quickly screwed the bulb into place.

Placing a shaky hand on his muscular forearm, Halina attempted to pry herself loose from his hold. But Cameron brought his other arm up and folded her even closer into his embrace. She felt the white-hot imprint of his body on hers—the hard thighs pressing her own, the narrow hips flanking her buttocks, the belt buckle digging into her waist.

For one brief, insane moment she welcomed the security she felt with his arms about her, and the perfect fit of their bodies. She leaned into his chest, marveling at the width that could so comfortably accommodate her. But her involuntary relaxation caused quite a different reaction in him, and Halina felt his unmistakable sign of arousal.

Flinching, she pulled urgently at his hands, fighting the feel of soft matted hair, rigid muscle, and the lingering aroma of lime after-shave that, combined with his male scent, assaulted her senses.

He didn't release her at once, but merely loosened his

hold as she struggled. Halina strove for composure and was relieved when her voice emerged relatively level.

"Game's over, Mr. Connors. You've had your fun. Now let me go."

She could feel his resistance in every taut line of the powerful male body. She thought he was going to ignore her request when he brought his head down and brushed his cool lips softly against the sensitive cords of her neck, parting them to suck some of her moist, salty flesh into his mouth. Shivers started racing along every nerve of her body, so she was barely aware when he slowly lifted his head, unlaced the fingers that covered her quivering stomach, and brought his hands around to rest for an instant on her rounded hips. With a ragged sigh, he dug his fingers into her soft curves and then put her away from him.

As soon as she was free, Halina whirled to face him.

"I think we'd better discuss your idle comment about discrimination, Mr. Connors. Had I not been a woman, you would not have thought twice about replacing your own bulb. Had you been another man, I'd have most graciously honored your request as soon as possible." She paused to gulp some fresh night air and continued heatedly, "Let's get one thing clear, Mr. Connors. I rented you an apartment in good faith, and this is not the way I want to be repaid." Seeing that he was about to interrupt, she sliced the air with her hand and cried, "No, I'm not finished. You were on the make tonight. And I do not appreciate wolves. I do think that I could at least expect more decency and civility from you."

"I think you're confusing decency with some basic natural drives," he said. "However," he went on quickly before she could intervene, "I do apologize for having you come over tonight on such a transparent excuse. But not for anything else."

Halina was not satisfied with his apology, but she knew from his unflinching stare that he'd meant what he said. At least he was honest, she told herself, and for some unknown reason the thought cheered her.

But it didn't mean he could get away with such tactics. For one thing, they had to keep a business relationship. For another, he was far more dangerous than Ted or Louis, or even Jeff, with whom she had once been in love. She was not about to let herself in for another rude awakening. Not ever again.

As she stepped past him, her body brushed accidentally against his. She felt the shock go through her to the tips of her toes, and moved hastily away from his jeans-and-T-shirt-clad body. She looked up to find a knowing glint in the smoldering green eyes.

Her resolve hardened even further, Halina told him as she stepped into the hallway, "I'll prepare a bag with each type of bulb you might need in the future. And should any other repairs prove necessary, please feel free to call in the appropriate specialist. I'll reimburse you. As I'm rather pressed for time lately, I'm sure it'll be the best solution."

He grinned, the play of white teeth against bronzed skin startling. "Coward," he murmured, the lazy sweep of his gaze over her perspired, disheveled body making her shift uncomfortably.

Although Halina felt heat rush into her face, she returned his look coolly. "Not at all, Mr. Connors. Only not young and foolish. Nor ready to play in a tournament where I'm out-experienced."

She saw surprise and admiration cross his features before she turned and headed for the door, ignoring the husky voice saying, "It's Cam. Not Mr. Connors," as she let herself out of his apartment.

Walking quickly down the hall, Halina tried to shake off not only Cameron's charged presence, but her own strong reaction to him. Not since her disillusionment with Jeff had she felt so affected by a man. With Louis her feelings had been more tepid—the main reason, she saw now, for her inability to respond to his lovemaking.

Her father had managed to help her over the hurt, humiliation, and rage she'd experienced at eighteen, and Halina had been able once again to look at men as individuals. Imperfect, but still human beings, she'd told her best friend Lorraine often enough, in irritated response to Lorraine's blind adoration of the male sex.

But the wounds had obviously gone deeper than she'd thought. For the cool demeanor she'd developed, and that had served her well for so long, did not seem to suffice in keeping Cameron Connors at bay.

Opening the door to her apartment with unsteady fingers, Halina felt her muscles shivering from exhaustion, and her mind was charged with visual and tactile images that made her entire body tingle. She leaned against the door for a moment, breathing deeply, welcoming its cool solidity against her heated skin.

Straightening with an effort, she went into the bathroom and let the water run for her bath while she prepared an ice-cold lemonade to ease the dry tightness of her throat. Her appetite had deserted her, and her hands were still trembling as she poured the freshly squeezed juice into a tall glass, vowing that she'd be doubly careful with Cameron Connors in the future.

He'd succeeded where others had failed the last few years: He'd forced her to recognize her own needs and his attraction. The fact that he'd not been discouraged as easily as the others, whom she'd frozen with a stare or a well-chosen phrase, frightened her.

Cameron Connors had awakened dormant feelings she'd thought safely under control. And, Halina told herself grimly, she was not going to give up her pleasant, comfortable, and peaceful life for anyone.

Especially not for Cameron Connors.

Chapter

3

THE HEAT IN the dining room was suffocating, but Halina resisted the impulse to turn on the central air conditioning. She had opened all the windows that morning to let the stale air out and allow the reviving northern winds in. But at four in the afternoon her thermometer showed it was already 85—not 65, as had been the day's predicted high. And along with the heat came the sticky mugginess that was all too common for Chicago in July.

The day reminded her of the one when she had first met Cameron Connors. That had been three weeks ago, and he had not sought her out after the incident with the light bulb. Halina reflected that maybe her brush-off had worked. Determinedly she pushed all thoughts of her newest tenant from her mind.

Impatiently wiping her forehead with a tissue, Halina smiled in poignant remembrance of the time her father had first thought of installing central air conditioning in the building. He had owned two buildings at the time, and it had meant a big cash outlay, but the project had paid for itself in the past eight years. People were more willing to rent, and more apt to remain in a building with central air.

He had sold the other building five years ago, to ensure that Halina had enough money for graduate school. The rest of the money had gone to finance his part in an expedition into the Amazon. It had been the dream of a lifetime for her father, who held degrees in botany and biology.

But it had cost him his life.

Halina sighed, the wound of her loss exactly a year ago today not totally healed. Although her father had fulfilled his dream, the arduous three-week journey had precipitated his heart attack. He had continued simply on willpower after experiencing chest pains his second week out.

A man totally immersed in his research, he had reduced his teaching load to spend more time in the lab. But Hal Barkley had not been physically fit. Even a year later, Halina found she resented his premature death.

Perhaps he had sensed the end, because that last week he had told her he was now content. His only regret had been that he would be leaving her alone. But at least, he'd said, she'd be financially secure and had found her niche in the world.

Lately Halina was not so sure. If only her mother were still alive. . . . But Virginia Barkley had died when Halina was ten, the senselessly tragic victim of a drunk driver speeding on her side of the road. And her father had never really recovered, throwing himself even more furiously into his work, too busy for a growing daughter. She sometimes wondered whether her father's indifference had prompted her, as a sheltered eighteen-year-old, to accept Jeffrey Manford's charming, overwhelming attentions. Even now, though she was well into her twenties, it still hurt her to think that she had always come last in her father's life.

The knock on the door interrupted the flow of her memories, and Halina smiled with self-mockery. The intrusion had come just in time to prevent her from falling into a well of self-pity—something she despised. She brushed away the lone drop that had trailed a path down her dusty cheek and, taking a second to compose herself, went to answer the door.

Halina was surprised to see Cameron Connors, but even his presence was welcome to help banish the painful thoughts that kept invading her peace on this anniversary of her father's death.

Her voice was husky with repressed emotion as she greeted him, but she resolutely maintained her smile. "Good afternoon, Mr. Connors. Do you need anything?"

Halina saw a disturbing expression cross his features as he took in her appearance and then looked back up at her eyes, which she knew did not match her bright smile.

She backed up to allow him to step into the entry hall. She squirmed uncomfortably when he didn't say anything at first, but merely allowed his gaze to roam and then settle on her body for an inordinate time after she'd closed the door behind him.

"Should I step out again and allow you time to dress?" he asked with obvious reluctance.

As realization hit her in a rush, Halina tore her grandmother's apron off her body. She had opened the door and then kept her back against it, unmindful that the large apron hid her attire from view, making it appear as if the apron was the only thing she wore.

"I was afraid I'd caught you at a bad time," he added, but his mocking expression and glinting eyes that visually caressed the curves exposed to him belied the statement.

"Not at all," she managed, regretting having taken off the oversized bib apron, which had concealed her black tube top and brief white shorts. She looked down at the cup she was still holding and noticed that her knuckles were white from the strength of her grip. She forced her fingers to relax and said, "I was just cleaning the coffee service."

Cameron took the cup and examined the exquisite porcelain with twelve-karat gold surrounding the individual scenes. "It's a beautiful piece of work," he said as he gave it back to her.

Halina restored the cup to its proper place in the walnut china cabinet and explained, "Each piece depicts a different scene from *Tosca* and is an exact duplicate of an eighteenth-century baroque design. Most of the pieces in the cabinet belonged to my grandmother—as did the apron," she added.

He pointed to the large cuckoo clock on the wall, with its intricately carved deer head topping a pastoral scene. "The clock too?" he asked.

Halina nodded, closing the glass door of the cabinet carefully. "That's right. That particular clock is one hundred years old. It was a wedding present from my great-grandparents to my grandmother, who was born in Bavaria."

He leaned against a rocking chair placed to one side of the huge green-and-blue couch and asked with interest, "Then you're of German descent?"

"Only partly." Halina smiled warmly at the memory of her paternal grandmother, who had died when she was only eight. "My grandfather was a Canadian who was vacationing in California. He met my grandmother, who was also on vacation, in San Francisco. They both liked the Golden Gate City so much they decided to live in the States after they married. And my mother . . ." Here her voice broke, and Halina quickly walked to a chair and sat down, realizing she was more emotionally drained than she'd thought. "She was an exchange student from England who married her science professor—my father."

Realizing she'd been rambling, she cut herself off abruptly and motioned toward the couch. "But I'm sure you didn't come to hear my genealogy. What can I do for you?"

Cameron straightened and, going around the couch, sat down facing her. "You have a way of making a person forget what he wanted in the first place." He smiled. Halina waited for him to continue, ignoring his leading comment.

"Actually, I found myself at loose ends and I wondered if you would care to have dinner with me."

Her hand went absently to the thick braid resting on

one white shoulder and automatically pushed it away so that it rested against her back. She saw his eyes glint as he took in the way her full breasts strained the stretch material of her top, but Halina was too busy deciding how to answer his invitation to be irritated. She was amused at his offhandedness, but then, she couldn't expect more, since beyond the pass he'd made a week after he'd moved in, Cameron Connors had shown no interest in her. Just this past weekend she'd seen him go into his apartment with a stunning brunette.

Cameron apparently misinterpreted her indecision because he added, "I hope you'll let me repay you in some way for renting the apartment to me. I promise not to keep you out too late, and to behave like a true gentleman."

Halina smiled, his solemn entreaty making up her mind. The fact that he wanted to take her to dinner out of gratitude was certainly a change. She hadn't had much of a social life lately, and the notion of staying home with sad memories did not appeal in the least. Considering that most men she went out with seemed to lose their heads over her voluptuous figure, Halina thought it would be refreshing to go out with someone who wouldn't turn octopus on her. It would be a relief to have dinner with a man whose masculinity would not be threatened if she insisted on paying the tab to avoid paying the piper.

"I accept," she said. Then, at the relief that flickered in his green eyes, she added half-teasingly, half-warningly, "On condition that you keep your word."

Putting his hand over his heart, he drawled, "You got it, ma'am."

Halina felt the stirrings of misgiving at his wide grin. It seemed as if he'd been concerned about her answer, which was silly. He'd not approached her in two weeks.

Cameron got up and curved his large palm lightly around her bare shoulder. Halina frowned as she felt warmth travel from the spot he'd touched to deep within her body.

Leaning back to force his hand to drop away, Halina asked in a cooler voice, "Something else, Mr. Connors?"

"You really look like a teacher now, Halina. All prim and disapproving," he said in a tone laced with amusement. His eyes gleamed as her dark eyebrows rose haughtily, and he added, "Since I'm not familiar with many restaurants in Chicago, I thought you could perhaps suggest one. Unless you'd be interested in the Ninety-fifth, or the revolving one near O'Hare?"

There had been an odd note in his voice, and she found it hard to believe that he usually left such decisions as picking a restaurant to his date. But that was it, she told herself. She was *not* his date. He didn't seem anxious to take her to a romantic setting like the 95th at the top of the Hancock, and Halina was not so inclined herself. She'd been to these places with Jeff, and tonight she wanted to escape all painful memories, not revive them. "Are you fond of German food, Mr. Connors?" she asked.

"Yes, but I haven't had it very often," he answered easily.

"Then why don't we try Math Igler's?"

"Home of the singing waiters?"

"Yes, but they have waitresses also now. How did you know of it?"

"I was born in Chicago," he told her, "and went to grammar school here for a few years before my parents moved to Texas." While Halina was digesting this rather startling information, he added, "I'll make a reservation. Okay if I pick you up at six-thirty?"

"Fine," Halina answered absently as he let himself out.

She went over to lock the door and leaned against it for a while as she mentally reviewed and discarded outfits for the evening.

* * *

Halina put the finishing touches to her hair, which she'd intricately twisted atop her head. Tiny curls escaped at the sides and back, and reflected the overhead light like burnished walnut.

The mirror above her dresser caught the sparkle of the silver comb she'd inserted on one side, and the brilliance of the silver pendants with their tiny diamonds— a high school graduation present from her father—which dangled daintily from her ears.

As she stood up and walked to the side of the wide brass bed where she'd placed her sandals, the silver chiffon rustled about her in a shimmering cloud. She looked at herself critically once more, liking the way the shirred bodice hugged her firm upturned breasts and narrow waist. She had second thoughts for a moment, knowing that her full figure was displayed to its best advantage, but she brushed them aside. She was twenty-seven, after all.

Although she often wished for the long, lean look of a model, at times like these she was reasonably satisfied. Unlike her face, which she considered only moderately pretty, her figure, at least, Halina thought, was better then average.

The double spaghetti straps slid down her shoulder as she bent to put on her gold sandals, and she slipped them back up with impatient fingers. Her heels sank into the white shag carpeting, and as she left the bedroom, Halina struggled with the catch on her wristwatch, which had been causing her problems lately. She had meant to take it to the jeweler's when it had first begun to stick, but had never gotten around to it.

She had almost given up when the solution presented itself. She would go to Cameron's door and ask him to fasten it. She was beginning to feel rushed. Although it was only six-fifteen, she'd never played the game of being late for a date. She appreciated punctuality and honesty in a person, and didn't think it fair to let a man cool his heels when he had probably rushed to be on time.

Taking a lace shawl from the closet, Halina picked up her clutch purse and turned off the lights as she crossed the room. Opening the door, she took a step—only to stop when she spied a striking fortyish blonde coming out of Cameron Connors's apartment.

"Thank you, darling. You've been a dear to fit me into your schedule at the last minute." The sultry voice broke into a deep, seductive laugh. "I'll be sure to recommend you to all my friends."

Halina retreated hastily. She hadn't made out what Cameron Connors said, because his voice had a deeper timbre and was muffled by the walls, but she did hear the husky chuckle that met the blonde's last words. His door closed and Halina remained statue-like inside her own doorway, hidden from the blonde, who undulated her phenomenal figure down the hallway on stiletto heels that matched the flame-colored backless jumpsuit. The chic sophistication written in capital letters in the expensive hairdo and equally prohibitive clothes, plus the diamonds circling both wrist and neck, flattened Halina's earlier elation.

Halina closed the door slowly and went into the living room, turning on the lamp and dropping her watch on the end table. She sat down on the couch, absently clutching her purse and shawl in her lap, pondering what she'd just witnessed.

Apparently Cameron had other fish to fry, as evidenced by the brunette and now the blonde. And what fish! She smiled wryly, still dazzled by the vision of wealth, beauty, and chic poise. It could be the reason Cameron had not sought her out. And to think she had thought her words had dissuaded him.

The woman's reference to his schedule puzzled her. She had not been aware that Cameron had found a job. And if the woman visited him at the apartment, that meant he worked at home. Perhaps he was an accountant.

Shaking her head at the way she was trying to fit the puzzle that was Cameron Connors together, Halina admonished herself that it was really none of her business. Getting up from the couch, she draped the shawl over her arm and resolutely walked to the door. She had looked forward to the evening out, and she wasn't going to let anything spoil it.

Chapter

4

"THAT WAS TERRIFIC," Cameron said with a satisfied sigh as he leaned back from the table, his torso dwarfing the straight back of the chair.

Halina delicately wiped a corner of her mouth with the white linen napkin, her preoccupied eyes glancing briefly at the breathtakingly virile man lounging so casually across from her.

Not knowing what to expect, Halina had felt somewhat uncomfortable as they left Barkley Court in her car. When Cameron Connors had showed up at her door just as she reached it, she had wanted to ask him what he did for a living and who exactly that fortyish blonde had been.

But as Cameron's landlady, she had no right to pry into his private life. Her tenants knew that she considered each apartment a separate entity. She'd never invade their privacy.

It was her strong curiosity about the man sitting opposite her that had thrown her off kilter. She hadn't expected ever to feel any deep interest in another man. The ones she usually dated, though nice and secure enough, certainly did not elicit any sort of speculation. Their primary appeal was that they did not demand from her more than she was ready to give.

Nervously folding the napkin, she set it down next to her empty plate and drew her eyes away from the wide expanse of chest covered by a hand-tailored black jacket.

Halina found she resented Cameron's easy charm and

intelligent conversation. She'd been determined to enjoy herself—and now she found that she'd taken on more than she wanted to handle. And her own personal code, which forbade her to get the answers to the questions burning in her mind, did not make her feel any better.

"I must say, it's been a while since I've seen such an expression of displeasure on a woman's face over a dinner table. Am I that hard to take?"

Halina looked at him blankly for a moment. His grin widened, and she found she was not immune to the unmitigated sensuality of it. "I think my ego is in serious danger of being permanently totaled," he told her in a voice whose seductive power matched his smile.

Forcibly pulling her mind and senses into a coherent working unit, Halina responded to his teasing statement. "Your ego couldn't be dented—let alone damaged—if I tried my best."

"Don't be so sure of that."

The glint in his green gaze disconcerted her and, grabbing her wineglass, she took a sip and rearranged her full skirt before leaning back in her chair.

"My Veal Goulash with spetzel was delicious. How was your Sauerbraten?"

His low rich chuckle vibrated across the table and draped itself around her. "My sauerbraten and potato pancakes were great," he answered dutifully, then added, "but I'm sure we can find a more titillating topic of conversation."

Halina studied the ruby liquid in her glass. When she lifted her gaze to Cameron's, her eyes were the cold gray of the gleaming silverware.

"I'm not here to titillate you, Mr. Connors. You invited me because you were at loose ends, and I accepted because I thought the nature of our relationship was clear to you: strictly business." A combustible silence followed; then she added on a maternal tone she knew would set his teeth on edge, "I should think you would have been taught better manners, and the proper way to express gratitude."

Halina felt no remorse about bringing up the fact that she had done him the favor of allowing a short-term rental. He had promised to behave, but was reverting to his true colors. And Halina wanted Cameron Connors under control—if such a thing was possible. She was finding him too attractive, and did not want to combat both his pursuit and her irrational response.

"Lady, we don't have a relationship. Period."

His checked explosion startled her. Although his posture remained relaxed, she could see a muscle working in the angular jaw.

"Were you expecting one?" she shot back, again visualizing that gorgeous creature leaving Cameron's apartment.

"That would be an impossible mission," he said, his eyes narrowing to malachite slits. "You have the turtle's knack for withdrawing into your shell at the slighest hint that your turf might be invaded."

"And doesn't that give you a hint?" she asked calmly. "I like my life the way it is," she told him when he remained silent, his face impassive again except for the slight pulse jumping under the bronzed skin of his left temple. "And I don't appreciate rudeness, interference, or tasteless, meaningless come-ons."

Taking another sip of wine, ignoring the excitement she felt rushing through her veins at the sight of those wonderous green eyes, Halina added silkily, "With the tactlessness you've just revealed, though, I'm surprised you even get to first base."

"You'd better keep in mind that I'm used to home runs, Halina Barkley," he warned on a slightly menacing note.

Halina smiled confidently. Although she was attracted to Cameron, she had proved immune to men in the past—especially Cameron's kind. True, he was a notch above all the other men she'd met since Louis, but as long as she kept her guard up, she would be able to deal with Cameron's brand of aggressive masculinity.

"Do you achieve your remarkable record by comparing the women you take out to turtles?"

As she uttered the words, Halina's sense of the ridiculous reestablished itself, and her mouth curved. Cameron's mouth twitched also, and they both laughed, their quickly developing hostility fading under the force of their mirth.

"Would you like some dessert?" he asked when she'd recovered her breath.

"No, thank you. But if you like beer," she said, eyeing the large mug in front of Cameron, "you'll probably like the section of the show that's coming up next."

When they announced the beer contest and asked for volunteers, Halina raised her hand, blithely volunteering Cameron. He climbed onto the small stage that took up part of one side of the restaurant and proceeded to down an enormous jug of beer in the least time, beating out the other men and one woman who had participated. After that there were contests involving pipe smoking and yodeling. Then, much to Halina's chagrin, one of the singers singled her out, telling her he remembered her from when she had come in regularly in years past, and urged her onto the stage.

Halina, whose voice tended to break on high notes, and whose German had fallen into disuse, tried unsuccessfully to get out of her predicament. Not only did she dislike the limelight, but she had an aversion to making a fool of herself, and she resented the singer's excellent memory.

But the fun-loving clientele, who urged her on at the singer's insistence, and Cameron's amused comment that turnabout was fair play had her climbing the stage in trepidation, reluctantly searching her memory for the German lyrics. She was thankful when they switched to

English after a few renditions in which her voice seemed to take its own path away from the established harmony. When everyone was invited to join the sing-along, Halina walked down the steps and headed to her table with the air of someone reprieved from a death sentence.

Halina sank into her chair somewhat sheepishly. She'd managed to get into the spirit of things through sheer willpower, but could not totally recapture the innocent enthusiasm she'd had as an undergraduate. She had never been an extrovert, but circumstances had made her a more private person as the years went by, and she had found that climbing onto that stage had been harder than she'd anticipated.

Cameron seemed to sense her discomfort, because he covered her trembling hand with his and told her gently, "You were terrific, you know. You have a sexy voice."

Halina laughed shakily and told him, "That's another way of saying my voice could probably sharpen nails."

Cameron chuckled, shaking his head. "Not so. It's an unusual voice." He ignored her snort and added, "Besides, I'm sure the men were too busy looking at your nonvocal—attributes to worry much about your vocal cords."

"Thanks a lot! There are women here too, you know," she said, amused.

"But none as beautiful as you."

Halina was jarred by the quiet words, which held the ring of conviction. Although she tried to tell herself that the compliment was probably a well-practiced line, she found that it affected her deeply. Cameron obviously liked women—she hadn't needed to see him with the blonde and brunette to learn that. It was written in the way he'd spoken to her, acted toward her. And although one part of her was disturbingly glad that Cameron was not completely the stereotypical wolf she despised, another part was worried that beneath the apparent wealth and obvious good looks lay a man who could penetrate her so-far-impregnable defenses.

More subdued now, Halina suggested they leave, and Cameron agreed. She could tell he had noticed her change in mood and wanted to say something. But he apparently changed his mind, because he took care of the bill and, gripping her elbow firmly, led her out of the restaurant and into the beautiful starry summer night.

After a long, leisurely walk down the Magnificent Mile, Michigan Avenue, they decided to go up to the top of the John Hancock Center. The lobby, as usual, was crowded and they had to wait for an elevator.

But Halina knew the wait and the good-natured jostling had been worth it when they stepped off the elevator, Cameron's arm protectively around her shoulders. As they approached the window, she felt she was suspended in the clouds. The dark mystery of the lake was punctuated by bobbing boats that winked their illumination up to the top of the more than one-hundred-story building.

Cameron had suggested a drink in the lounge while they waited for the elevator. But Halina did not want to resurrect memories of the times she and Jeff had come to celebrate his victories in basketball. His parents had been wealthy, proud of their youngest son and his status as captain of the team. And Jeff had taken advantage of their frequent travel to use his parents' apartment in Marina City in their absence. He had ignored Halina's timid requests that they try the Lincoln Park Zoo, or a picnic, or horseback riding, demanding instead that she dress up and they go out in style. And, she remembered, it had been at his parents' luxuriously appointed apartment that she had given herself to Jeff for the first time after a subtly escalated courtship. His cruel words still rang in her ears, and she wished she could wipe that incident from her memory as easily as Jeff had wiped her out of his life. . . .

Cameron's voice threaded through her bitter musings,

and Halina realized that he'd been trying to get her attention for a while.

"Do you do this often?" he asked with amusement that held a tinge of exasperation.

Halina was surprised at the strength with which these memories held her tonight; she had built an ordered, actively satisfying life in which the past was seldom allowed to intrude.

"Do what?" she asked, grateful for the intimate darkness of the observation deck, which hid the guilty flush of her cheeks.

"Go off into a world by yourself," Cameron answered with definite irritation now.

Halina smiled in relief, the remembered pain receding with the impact of his forceful personality, even as she realized from his tone that Cameron was not used to women ignoring his presence.

"There you go again, with that 'Mona Lisa' smile," he accused as they began walking again and the lights of a nearby skyscraper reflected for an instant on her face. Confirming her guess, he added in a low, intense voice, "I don't particularly like being disregarded, and I don't think I have to remind you that that is also a breach of good manners on a date."

Halina stiffened and stopped walking. She leaned against the handrails, glad that she did not suffer from vertigo. Gazing at the houses, streets, cars, and trees along the Loop, which formed a chiaroscuro configuration, she reminded him gently, "But I'm not your *date*, am I, Mr. Connors?"

"Come on, now. Cut that Mr. Connors nonsense," he interjected.

"One of the reasons I agreed to come out with you tonight is that you made it clear you had nothing more interesting to do, and you wanted to express your gratitude." She paused for breath and turned to look at him, leaning her elbow on the railing. "I'm tired of going out to dinner and battling for the check. Either way it's a hassle: if I insist on paying, a tug-of-war ensues because my escort fears for his masculinity; if I let him pay, I'm expected to recompense him."

"So you thought I'd be safe," he stated dryly, fairly spitting out the last word as if it contaminated him.

"I did." She raised her chin a fraction. "But if this is the way you express your gratitude, I shudder to think how you treat your enemies."

Cameron was silent for a long moment, studying her in the half gloom. Halina could feel the frustration hardening his body. But why should he be upset? She had agreed to go out with him tonight only on the condition that things be kept impersonal. She was satisfied with her life as it was for the most part, and she knew that if she let the feelings she had kept in hibernation for so long thaw out, only pain could result. It would be madness to become addicted to Cameron's careless charm. Halina had learned her bitter lessons.

"Where would you like to go dancing?"

His words sounded so innocuous that Halina blinked in surprise, trying to adjust to the unexpected question.

"The Drake is only a couple of blocks away," she ventured. "But what about your promise to take me home early?"

"The night's still young," he answered smoothly. "And the promise still holds. You set the time when the evening ends."

Halina considered her options. If she went home now, she would not be able to sleep yet, and her old memories would still haunt her. On the other hand, Cameron was proving to be dangerously pleasant company. . . .

"All right," she decided. "But on one condition."

"Another one?" Cameron asked in a voice threaded with irony. "You should have been a lawyer. But okay, let's hear it."

"I want to go to a park that's nearby. It should be

deserted, in case you don't care to be seen in a children's playground."

His answer somehow did not surprise her. "I don't give a damn what other people think. If it will make you happy, then by all means, let's go."

The short walk was accomplished in companionable silence. Halina appreciated not being forced to make small talk. She had wanted to enjoy the quiet beauty of the summer night, and somehow Cameron must have sensed her mood, giving her a welcome few minutes of silence.

When they reached the park, it was indeed empty, the playground section a bit mysterious now under the silvering moonlight, the trees creaking slightly in the cool lake wind. The shadows they cast formed curious mobile shapes.

Halina headed straight for the swing set, lost in the impulse, giving no thought to her elegant dress. She wanted to put all reflection on the past away, if even for a short while, and she twirled the chains around, watching with childish delight as two swings spun in mad tandem.

She turned to Cameron, who was leaning against one of the posts supporting the swings, regarding her with a lazy smile, and asked with contained excitement, "Would you mind pushing?"

Although outwardly calm, Halina found herself anxiously awaiting his answer. But Cameron didn't demur, nor make nasty remarks, as Jeff had done one afternoon when she'd convinced him after a lot of arguing to take her to one of the parks by the lake.

Cameron straightened slowly and walked to her side. "No, I don't mind. But it will cost you," he drawled as he took off his jacket and rolled up the sleeves of his lightweight beige shirt.

"Well, let me consider this first," Halina said laughingly.

"You've missed your profession," he said with lazy amusement. At her raised brows, he elucidated, "You should be conducting auctions or presiding over garage sales."

"Look who's talking," she responded lightly, amazed that she was able to engage in such teasing with Cameron. "You were the one who insisted on barter, and I'd like to know what you expect in return before I make a commitment."

"Cautious, aren't we?"

"I am," she returned pertly.

Cameron calmly took a white silk handkerchief and cleaned the seat of the swing before opening the cloth and spreading it across the wood.

"I think a kiss should do it," he said unexpectedly, and Halina almost jumped, startled out of her fascinated contemplation of Cameron's deft movements and the tensile strength of his beautiful long-fingered hand.

"Fine," she agreed readily, surprising Cameron with her easy compliance. Then she added, "On the condition, of course, that, since you're doing the pushing, I'll do the kissing."

"Another condition." Cameron groaned, and Halina jumped in helpfully, "Unless you'd like me to push you in return?"

"No, thanks," he answered dryly as he held the swing for her. "I like my trade better."

Gathering up her flowing silver skirt, Halina asked impishly, "But under my terms?"

"Under your terms."

Halina felt his strong hands grab her waist as he pulled her back against his chest, holding her aloft for an inordinate time. "You seem to have your own style of pushing."

His hands increased their pressure, fingers digging deeper but not painfully into her sides as he pulled her higher off the ground. Then she was released suddenly, and the sensation of soaring freedom was delightful.

As she was borne back, he answered smoothly, "You didn't specify which way you wanted to be pushed. So I'm just using some creativity."

His hands closed briefly about her hips this time, and on her return, they clasped her slightly above her waist.

Halina found herself trying to guess the next position of his hands, and she discovered she was anticipating his touch each time her swing went back as much as she was savoring the soothing, invigorating motion itself.

She gave herself entirely to the experience. She remembered that Jeff had always made her feel immature, had belittled any spur-of-the-moment suggestion she'd made. He'd enticed her to bed by playing on her loneliness, on her feelings for him, and on the fact that she'd needed to prove her maturity. If only she'd realized at the time what she recognized much later: Jeff was a taker. He'd never given anything in return, aside from empty materialistic gifts. So easy—all he'd had to do was buy them. Perhaps that had been his main problem—his parents had made everything so effortless for him. He had killed her love and humiliated her, his insecurity making him strike out at anyone and anything.

By contrast, here was Cameron, coolly taking off his expensive jacket and rolling up his sleeves, as if pushing a woman in a park was an everyday occurrence.

"Higher, please," she asked, and he obligingly pushed her up into the cool night air, his hands sure and powerful as they boosted her even farther.

"More," she requested laughingly. "I'd like to reach the tree branch that seems just out of my grasp."

"Your wish is my command," he said huskily.

This time Halina was able to touch the leaves that had escaped her several times when they were caught in the capricious lake wind, and she exclaimed, "Eureka," forgetting everything for the moment as she let herself enjoy the play of the nocturnal breeze on her flesh. She leaned back until she was almost horizontal, her shining eyes taking in the solidity of the inverted masculine figure as she swung, her dress rustling and teasing her skin as it lifted and descended against her legs.

"You should do that more often," Cameron told her.

"Do what? Get on swings and act like a kid?" Her tone reflected some of the bitterness she'd tried to hide.

His voice was deep and gritty when he answered. "Laugh. Let yourself go."

Her legs lost their rigidity, brushing against the ground as she digested Cameron's words. She remembered what he'd said about her turtle shell, and knew it was true. She never allowed anyone to get too close. Nor did Halina ever permit all of herself to surface, especially when she dated. It had been a real slip on her part to show one side of the old Halina Barkley. And to Cameron Connors, of all people.

Hoping to divert his attention from her, Halina resumed swinging and asked him casually, "Have you settled in yet? Did you find a satisfying job?"

"Oh, no, you don't, Halina Barkley. No answers from me tonight. I have the feeling that if I tell you about myself, it'll be the last I see of you—figuratively speaking."

"What do you mean?" she asked, genuinely puzzled, getting a too-brief look at him on the return swing. His reversed features looked blurry with the moon partially hidden.

"You were planning on another disappearing act, weren't you?" he asked shrewdly. "You'd begun to let go, to show the vibrant, fun-loving Halina under that severe exterior. And now you're retreating into your comfortable shell."

"I told you before, I don't much like being compared to a turtle." How could the man get under her skin like this?

"Then don't act like one," he returned softly. "I'd like

to get to know the real Halina Barkley better."

"You make me sound like a split personality," she told him acerbically. "If I'm as repressed and bland as you've made me out to be, why bother to ask me out? Your gratitude can't be that great, nor do I believe you couldn't find anyone else to tie your 'loose ends' for you."

She heard his sharp intake of breath, but was not sorry she'd gone on the attack. Fear was not a pleasant sensation—and that was exactly what Cameron had inspired in her. He seemed able to tune in to her feelings, sometimes with frightening accuracy. Any knowledge Cameron gained of her would make her vulnerable. And Halina did not intend to be vulnerable again.

She could feel Cameron's eyes burning into her back as he let the swing slow, and she sensed that his relaxed demeanor was changing to sensual tension as her body encountered the muscular rigidity of his. His hands held her carefully by the waist before he set her free.

But when he spoke, his voice was cool and controlled. "Think you've had enough?"

Halina waited until the swing was almost still and then jumped off reluctantly, retrieving the handkerchief, which had slid off.

"Not really, but it's starting to get a bit cold." Walking over to him to give him the handkerchief, she asked him lightly, hiding her uncertainty, "Are you sure you don't want me to push you? I bet you haven't been on one of these in ages."

"Ages is right," he answered as he took the silk square. "But I'm afraid my weight might be too much, both for the swing and for you to push. You might weigh the same as a young boy, but my frame would strain the wood to its breaking point."

He stepped closer to her, swung his jacket about her shoulders, and pulled away the shawl tied loosely around her neck. "I don't think this will be of much help," he said as he folded it and put it over his shoulder. Halina had been about to protest that she didn't need the jacket, but both its warmth and masculine smell stopped her, and she decided she didn't mind the protective gesture after all. As a matter of fact, it had been so long since somebody had done something of that nature, she found she rather liked it.

"Want to try something else?" he asked, pointing to the exercise bars, the slides, and the seesaw, all painted bright yellow and orange.

"Not in this," she said, looking ruefully at her dress.

He smiled and put a casual arm about her shoulders as he led her out of the park. "I guess you're one of those people who like the simple things in life."

"Don't you?"

"I didn't used to," he replied slowly. "My parents went to Texas in search of the American dream. And I was caught up in their search." Cameron didn't say whether they'd succeeded, but Halina was sure they had. That made the fact that he seemed satisfied to be renting in her building all the more perplexing. And it raised the question of what Cameron himself was searching for.

"And now?" she prodded, unable to suppress the question that rose unbidden to her lips.

Halina could feel the bunching of his muscles as he deliberated about his reply. "I guess I'm in a transition period," he finally said, and this time she did not pursue the subject.

As disappointment washed over her, Halina realized she'd wanted Cameron to admit that he'd come to recognize that the simple things in life were the only ones worth having or pursuing. The only ones that lasted and gave any real satisfaction.

But as they turned onto Michigan Avenue again, seemingly one of dozens of loving pairs strolling quietly down the elegant street with its proliferation of flowers

and attractive boutiques, Halina was suddenly disgusted
with herself.

Despite her numerous self-warnings, she'd been hoping that Cameron would have values that paralleled hers.
She'd wanted Cameron to prove himself radically different from Jeff, despite—or perhaps because of—the
similarity of their wealthy backgrounds.

"Halina?"

His quiet voice brought her out of her reverie. He
drew her into a shadowy corner of a store entrance and
said throatily, "For the record, I don't find you bland. I
do believe you're deliberately repressing yourself, which
is a pity. I think the real Halina Barkley is a rich, exciting
personality with a lot to share. But I have no right to
pry"—his voice became lighter, mocking—"especially
as I intend to remain something of a mystery to you to
ensure that you see me again."

Before she could reply, he added quietly, "So I hope
you accept my apology. And I'm forfeiting my claim
until you feel that I deserve my reward."

Halina had never heard her father or Jeff say he was
sorry, and a knot suddenly formed in her throat. Standing
on tiptoe, she dropped a quick kiss on the rough, spicy
male cheek.

"I think a handsome apology like that deserves its own
reward."

"Does that mean I still have another kiss coming?"
he asked, his hands quickly going to her waist, no re-
pentance in tone or action now.

Halina laughed, the crystalline sound attracting the
stares of some passersby. "Sure, you can have another
peck on the cheek. But I think we'd better get out of
here. We're getting some very curious, interested looks."

His hands remained on her waist, his fingers rhythmically rubbing the thin material of her dress against her
skin.

"A woman who doesn't mind going to a park at night, disregarding her beautiful dress and any conventions, can't be worried about some curious looks."

Halina firmly removed his hands from her heated flesh and said wryly, "It's not only the looks I'm worried about."

"Well, that's better than calling me safe," he said silkily, following her slowly out of their temporary retreat.

"You're forgetting one thing," she reminded him with laughing eyes.

"Forgetting?" he asked, his arm finding its way around her waist again as he walked beside her on the street side.

"Your promise," she answered with amusement. "Or is your memory so short or conveniently forgetful that you've overlooked your promise to behave?"

He shook his head ruefully, pulling his jacket, which had begun to slide, up around her shoulders. "Remind me never to make another promise to you."

Halina shook her head in laughing denial and looked about her with pleasure, glad that a truce had been declared again.

She let her eyes feast on the great urban shopping mall, Water Tower Place; on Lewis Towers, the downtown campus of Loyola University; on the John Hancock, a huge steel-and-glass design spearing the night sky; and especially on the old Water Tower, her favorite Chicago landmark. The pseudo-Gothic creation, surrounded by imposing and spectacular skyscrapers, seemed to be a pool for all the light and attention, its clever illumination a golden beacon in the heart of a sophisticated city.

"Isn't it beautiful?" she exclaimed.

Cameron looked down at her with mixed surprise and amusement, apparently not sure what she was referring to.

"What is?"

His preoccupied tone indicated he'd been lost in deep thoughts of his own, and Halina made a wide sweep with her hand as she explained, "This. All around us. The city."

"You like Chicago?" he asked in some surprise.

"I *love* the city," she emphasized firmly. "A lot of people come here on business and all they really get to see is the crowded airport and impersonal hotels and conference rooms. But I think it's the most beautiful city in the country."

"Are you qualified to say?" he queried, obviously amused at her vehemence.

Halina had been asked that before when she defended her city to out-of-towners. "I've only been out of the States once, to Bermuda, but I've visited all fifty of them. And although San Francisco, New York, and San Antonio are also good-looking, I don't think any of them approach the architectural excellence and innovation of the Windy City."

They waited for the light at Chicago and Michigan and exchanged glances and smiles with other strolling couples. Halina felt somewhat of a fraud, because Cameron still had his arm draped about her shoulders. But when she'd tried to dislodge it earlier, he'd only increased the pressure and kept her body tightly molded into his warm hard side.

"It really irks me if visitors who only come in for a day or two, when there's winter slush, call it an ugly city, never having seen South Lake Drive, with its romantic walk, or Buckingham Memorial Park. Did you know it's patterned loosely after Versailles?" She stopped as a group emerging from Water Tower Place bumped laughingly into them, and Cameron pulled her to one side. "And it isn't only the city's imitative flair, like the Buckingham Fountain, with over a hundred jets of water. It's the metamorphosis the city has undergone, the architectural courage and genius that blends white marble, stainless steel, and tinted glass into a tasteful landscape."

"Do you work for the chamber of commerce?" Cameron asked, his mouth quirking.

"No," Halina answered, undaunted, her eyes bright as she admitted, "but I do volunteer work in the preservation of Chicago landmarks." She gave him her most innocent smile and asked ingenuously, "Would you like to hear about other unique, fascinating buildings? The Gothic Chicago Tribune Building, or the revivalist Preston Bradley Hall in the public library, or the Baha'i House of Worship . . ."

"Enough," Cameron protested, stopping in front of the Drake Hotel. Halina had been so absorbed in her descriptions, she'd barely noticed they'd reached it. "As much as I admire your expertise, I'm afraid I'm only interested in the functional aspect of a building."

"Philistine," she accused, now faced with the prospect of dancing with Cameron. It was bad enough he'd managed some breaks in her mental reserve. She was even more nervous about the inroads he could make with the intimacy of an evening of dancing.

"How about a walk along the beach?" she suggested.

Cameron groaned and, taking his jacket from her shoulders, shrugged into it. "I think I've done enough walking to last me a year."

He tried to guide her gently into the building, and when Halina held back, he asked mockingly, "What about your end of the bargain? The park for some dancing?"

Halina frowned, her mind scrambling for some way out.

"I'm not really feeling up to a walk along the beach. The wind is picking up," he added.

Remembering his unwell appearance the day she'd met him, Halina was immediately concerned and put her hand on his forearm. "You should have said something sooner. Do you want to go home? I don't really—"

"No, I'll be all right," Cameron interposed hastily,

putting his arm around her waist. "I'm not about to pass up the chance to hold all of you in my arms."

When Halina looked up at him reproachfully as they entered the hotel, Cameron grinned, his unrepentant humor again reminding her of the day she'd first seen him on her doorstep.

"Besides, this is one way I can be sure you won't ignore me, or go off into a world of your own."

Chapter

5

HALINA FOUND OUT to her dismay just how prophetic his statement was.

After securing a table for them in an intimate corner, away from the band, Cameron had led her onto the dance floor immediately, not even allowing her time for a drink. And although many of the couples were older, dancing ballroom style, Cameron had bypassed the customary hold and had put both hands around her waist.

As she looked around in some embarrassment, Halina noticed the amused and indulgent stares Cameron's aggressive and intimate grip elicited. But when she subtly tried to change to the traditional hold, Cameron calmly took her right hand in his left and wrapped both her arm and his around her waist, bringing her into even closer contact with his muscular thighs.

When a sharp tug only resulted in a painful twinge in her bent elbow, she hissed, "Let go of my arm," She took her other hand from his shoulder and tried to push at his chest, but the move proved ineffectual when Cameron closed the small gap between their upper torsos also and her hand was neatly trapped.

Giving her an amiable smile that she instantly distrusted, Cameron told her smoothly, "I'll let go of your arm eventually."

She waited expectantly, and when he didn't release her from the position, which was making her skin steam from her fury and his nearness, she cocked her head up at him.

"On one condition," he added, swaying gently in place. "I'd like to dance with you, but I'd rather do it as a shared activity. So if you just put your arms around my neck, we'll be all set."

His engaging grin did not disarm Halina. She was too incensed at the moment to respond to his playful charm. And if there was one thing she had not tolerated in her life the past few years, it was machismo.

"Then I guess you'll have to make it a single activity, because I'm calling your bluff. You can just drag me around the floor if you wish, for I most certainly will not be told what to do with my hands." For good measure, she added, "Nor any other part of my body."

When she saw the effect of her heated words on Cameron, she could have groaned aloud. Halina tried to maintain her ire as she saw his shoulders begin to convulse, knowing her temper was certainly her best defense against Cameron's devilish sense of humor. But she felt she was in imminent danger of breaking up too.

Cameron shook his raven head, his eyes sparkling with mirth, and his husky voice managed to convey both humor and passion in a headily potent combination Halina had not encountered before.

"We seem to be at a draw," he said. "Since we can't play a tie breaker to see who wins, why don't we just compromise?"

"By 'compromise' I assume you mean you let go of my hand and I put my arms around you as you wanted in the first place?" she asked with amusement.

"You must agree that if you hadn't been so difficult from the beginning, we would be circling around this dance floor a second time," he said with typical male logic.

"Me, difficult?" she returned belligerently, but the real fire was gone and Cameron seemed to sense it, for a tiny glow of masculine triumph shone in the green eyes. "As you said, we're stalemated, and I suggest we return to the table." Her customary common sense and combativeness had rescued her, but in this instance, she did not feel at all victorious.

Cameron read the determination in her face, but though he loosened his grip, he didn't release her entirely. As the strains of the "Blue Danube" faded softly away, the haunting melody of "Tales From the Vienna Woods," her favorite waltz, filled the air of the velvet-and-crystal room. Her feet began to move of their own accord, and Cameron shifted his hold as he led her lightly and expertly into perfectly executed turns. Halina felt the full skirt balloon, and faces and tables blurred as she gave herself up to the joy of dancing. When the waltz ended, she was acutely disappointed, and realized with a start she'd not danced with such pleasure, abandoning herself totally and trustingly to the beautiful music and to the care of a partner, since the last time she'd danced with her father, years ago.

"I was wondering how long it would take for you to succumb," Cameron told her with a self-satisfied air. When Halina gave him a puzzled look, he explained with cheerful aplomb, "I noticed your record collection had an unusual number of waltz albums in it."

"You fiend," she whispered in reluctant admiration. "You took a chance, though. They could just as well have belonged to my father."

"If you hadn't really liked them, you'd have put them away during this past year," he returned confidently.

Halina, who had been lulled into complacency after descending from the high of the timeless music, stiffened in his arms, belatedly noticing that they were around her waist and hers were loosely clasped to his upper arms. Cameron had been too smart to press his advantage and was holding her lightly, leaving a nonthreatening inch or so between them.

"What did you mean by 'this past year'?" she asked softly, giving him a dazzling smile that was apparently so unexpected, he momentarily lowered his guard.

"The time since your father's..." he began, then stopped abruptly as he realized his mistake. The smile fled Halina's pale face and his arms tightened around her waist, drawing her bruisingly against his unyielding length even as she attempted to escape.

"You knew today was the anniversary of my father's death," she said flatly, lowering her eyes swiftly from the compassion she read in Cameron's level gaze.

"Yes."

His answer didn't surprise her, but what did amaze her was the stab of pain she felt. "I'd like to leave, please," she requested in a dull voice.

"No!" His forceful monosyllable brought her head up again, and resentment began to smolder alongside the pain inside her. "You needed to get out tonight," he told her, ignoring the accusation in her eyes, "and if you go home now, no purpose will have been served."

"You mean there was a purpose behind that innocent-sounding invitation?" she asked silkily. Seeing he was about to object, she anticipated him and added cuttingly, "Of course. How stupid of me. I should have known better than to trust a man." Especially you, she added silently, feeling a new fissure in her defensive wall.

Cameron's hands dug into her spine at her last words, but his low voice was calm. "I don't know what kind of experiences you've had with men in the past, and I couldn't care less. They have no bearing on the present, and it seems to me you should get rid of that giant chip weighing down your exquisite shoulder."

While Halina looked at him in cold, silent anger, he added in a more conciliatory tone, "One of the worst things to get through is the anniversary of the death of a loved one. I know. My grandmother died four years ago, and I still miss her."

When Halina's glance remained hostile, he added with

gentle sarcasm, "I know you'll find this hard to believe, but men have feelings too."

Halina felt the bite of his rebuke, but she could not excuse his deception. "How did you know about my father?"

"Randolph told me." She stiffened in surprise, since Randolpy Que believed in privacy and it was hard to visualize him confiding anything to anyone, let alone a new tenant. But Cameron misunderstood her involuntary action and told her quietly, "He didn't suggest that I take you out, if that's what's bothering you. He merely mentioned the anniversary, maybe as a hopeful hint. The evening was entirely my idea."

"Well, hurrah for you! You've done your good boy scout deed for the week."

The silence that followed her bitter words stretched the tension until Halina felt her nerves would snap. What made it all the more painful was that she already regretted them. Goodness knew, Cameron was no saint. But he, like Randolph, had obviously meant well. Swallowing her pride, she opened her mouth to apologize, but Cameron forestalled her, saying bluntly, "Randolph happens to care a lot about you, as do all the people in your building. And you are *not* an object of pity."

Halina barely moved to the slow music as Cameron once more set their bodies in motion, evidently becoming aware that their standing interlude was a bit too conspicuous on the suddenly crowded floor. She was shocked at his ability to walk into her mind and zero in on her main objection. And the way he'd checked his own flare of temper showed her once more that she had underestimated him.

"You're right. I apologize. It was a nice thought to take me out tonight," she said, but could not resist adding, "even if it was on an evening when you were at loose ends."

Cameron laughed as she threw his own words back at him. "That rankled, did it? But would you have come out with me tonight if I had made it clear that this was a date? Or that I knew what today meant to you?"

Again he knew the workings of her mind, at least on one level, and it suddenly occurred to her that the reason could be that they thought alike. The possibility was so disturbing that she hurried into speech.

"Who could resist a fellow like yourself? And such a *charmingly* phrased invitation?" She smiled playfully. The tension of the past few minutes slowly drained from her body, and she relaxed within his possessive embrace.

Cameron folded her more closely into his length and guided her hands away from his shoulders, settling them once more around his neck. Halina felt his knees and thighs brush against her in his sensual sway to the ballad, and as her hands curled into the springy softness of his black hair, the peaks of her breasts flattened against the wall of his chest.

As she felt the tips press against the suddenly prickling satin of her bra, Halina prayed Cameron would not feel her entirely normal female response to his unsettling virility. But his harsh intake of breath told her he'd noticed, even through the barriers of her dress and his shirt. The hands that had been resting lightly on her hips moved around her narrow waist to interlock in the small of her back, and he instinctively pressed her close to the surging hardness of his thighs.

Halina's breathing became shallow and rapid, as fast as the pulse that ticked in her throat and that raced even faster when his lips descended to the spot and his tongue briefly flicked it. Her insides screamed and her legs went rubbery, her body melting under hands that shaped her frame to his as if they were complementing parts of a sensual puzzle.

The strains of one song dissolved into the next, and as more and more younger people came onto the dance floor, the renditions seemed to be increasingly ballads, which probably suited Cameron just fine, Halina suspected. If she had been honest with herself—something she was not very disposed to at the moment—she'd have admitted that it suited her quite well also.

The minutes sped by in a dreamy mist, the lights dimmed so that faces became indistinct, and Halina found she was fast losing all the control she'd worked so hard for these past years. She remembered how she'd known Cameron would represent trouble for her when he'd first shown up at Barkley Court such a short time ago and how complacently she'd dismissed his threat, convinced she had a special immunity that would enable her to handle him with ease.

But now she was being exposed to the full barrage of his charm, and her years spent deprived of exciting male company were taking their toll.

The fire in his eyes darkened to jade, and he removed his arms from her lower back to take her hands. Placing them around his waist, he teased softly, "I think this is more your height."

Halina had always been unhappy with her average height, but tonight she didn't mind his observation. Perhaps because his teasing voice held a caressing quality. Or maybe because she was so enmeshed in the sensual spell the man had created that she was going soft in the head, she scolded herself. But when he pressed her pliancy to his accommodating hardness, all rational thought fled again.

The new position was infinitely more comfortable, and Halina breathed in the lingering after-shave fragrance and the scent that was all Cameron with relaxed abandon. She vaguely noticed that they were still in the same intimate corner, away from the band and from stronger lighting. There had been no more waltzes or fox-trots since the younger crowd had taken over the floor, and so Cameron had staked out his territory and held her through several dances within its small limits.

"You've demonstrated you know how to dance quite well," she began deliberately. Cameron shifted his head a fraction to look down at her, and she added softly, "So don't you think we should move to where we can dance?"

He smiled lazily at the mocking inflection on the last word and drawled. "And what is wrong with this place? Or our dancing?"

Her eyes laughing at him, she asked scoffingly, "You call this dancing?"

"I don't think it's changed much since its pagan beginnings," he said, his hands rubbing tiny circles on her lower spine. "It still gets men and women together and meshes their need for music with their need for closeness."

"Well, we certainly can't get much closer," she admitted wryly, glancing down at their interlocked bodies. With her arms around Cameron's waist, their lower torsos were practically fused, and a fire she'd thought extinguished licked in her loins.

One of his hands left the small of her back to trace erotic patterns up and down her spine, causing chill bumps to rise in her soft flesh. "I had a feeling this would be the best way to get under those protective layers shrouding you."

Halina tensed at his words. "You mean you planned to come dancing tonight," she stated rather than asked, hoping he would deny any premeditation.

He seemed to be alert to every nuance of her body when he ordered softly, "Look at me."

Halina responded reluctantly to the quiet urgency of his tone and slowly lifted her gaze to his.

"If you mean 'plan' as in a big seduction scene—no, I didn't plan it. I credit you with too much intelligence for that." Halina wanted to see his words as a smooth, practiced line, but the patent sincerity of his eyes and voice precluded it. "I know, of course, from your piano and records that you like music. And when I saw the sheer pleasure you derived from the songs at the restaurant, and how you began to drop your guard a bit, I knew I wanted to go dancing with you tonight."

Halina continued to regard him with suspicion, but his next words banished the last of her protective rigidity.

"I just had to hold you in my arms tonight."

Halina sighed. Marshaling her considerable inner resources, she told him in a soft but firm voice, "I'd like to go home now."

"Right now?" he asked, black brows rising in puzzlement. He obviously had not missed the thread of disappointment running through her words, or the lack of resistance in her body. She *was* sorry—more than she'd have believed possible—but he'd already breached too many of her defenses for one night.

"Yes."

He put her away from him slightly and stopped dancing to tip her chin upward, but she refused to meet his gaze when he tried to decipher her apparent ambivalence by looking into her eyes.

But they lowered automatically, and then flew to his, when Cameron told her softly, "At least give me a minute to recuperate. My state is too painfully obvious right now."

Halina felt warm color steal into her cheeks, and her eyes wandered in limbo for a flustered moment. She dared not look below his belt again, nor did she want to meet his gaze, which she was sure would be filled with laughter.

While she berated herself for allowing him to throw her off balance, she perversely wished he would not hold her so far from the hard warmth of his body. Hers seemed to have a mind of its own, and she needed all her willpower not to sway toward his magnetic pull.

"Is your condition restored to normalcy?" she asked him in what had been intended as a cool tone but came out a throaty whisper.

"'Fraid not," he retorted, eyes gleaming. "Only you could really do that."

Her sense of humor had dispelled her previous awkwardness, and Halina was once more able to deal with the situation. Her ability to cope with troublesome moments had never deserted her before meeting Cameron.

Giving him a frank, direct stare, she said, "Come now, Mr. Connors. Surely you can do better than that. I seem to have heard that line before."

"And obviously had a smart, appropriate reply each time you heard it, didn't you?" he said dryly, his glance raking her face with open, undisguised hunger.

The light in her eyes dimmed abruptly. "All but once," she murmured in a brittle tone. "And that's all it takes, isn't it?" Disengaging herself swiftly, she said, "Shall we go?"

She preceded him quickly to their table, but his long legs brought him to her side as she was ready to leave.

Grabbing hold of her arm, he asked lightly, "You know, of course, that it's not proper to leave a gentleman on the dance floor?" But the penetrating glance that seemed to be dissecting her into minute parts was anything but light.

"As you're neither a gentleman nor were you at all proper on the dance floor, the question does not arise, does it?" she said with honeyed sweetness.

Cameron didn't reply. Leading her in silence through the deep-carpeted lobby, out of the hotel into the cool night air, he ignored her protests and once again slid his jacket over her bare shoulders.

As they walked down Michigan Avenue, still beautifully lit and alive though its sounds were somewhat muted at this advanced hour, Cameron asked, "Would you like to tell me about that one experience that has apparently soured you on the rest of the male sex?"

Fighting down her heightened awareness of him, Halina almost hugged the buildings at her left as she strode silently, berating herself for her slip about Jeffrey and hoping he would take the hint when she didn't answer. She had gone out with Cameron to avoid memories, not recount them.

As they entered the John Hancock Building, where the car was parked, and waited for the elevator, Halina began to breathe a bit easier, thinking he'd given up. She was not up to talking about Jeff tonight and Cameron didn't have the right to ask.

But as soon as the door swished to a close and the elevator shot upward smoothly, Cameron leaned close to her. The cubicle was suddenly suffocatingly small.

Propping himself on an elbow that brushed her shoulder, he asked with quiet insistence, "Why don't you want to talk about it? What has given you such a distrustful view of life?"

Halina tried to edge away, instinctively resisting his appeal and the velvet quality of his voice. But his hand followed her slight movement and his fingers closed lightly about the back of her neck.

"I'd rather not."

Halina found she was incapable of escaping his magic web. She felt paralyzed. Paradoxically, her body had never been more alive—though achingly so.

The timbre of his voice, low and rough, rumbled in the small space. "I'm a good listener."

Just when she thought she'd surely succumb to the spell he'd cast with his touch, voice, and eyes, the door opened, and Halina moved jerkily past him. She breathed in the cool, revitalizing air and welcomed the relative openness of their parking level as a convict would relish the space just outside prison upon his release.

Halina spotted her car right away and walked automatically toward it. They had taken her car because he didn't have one; when she asked him why not, he'd made a joke about preferring beautiful chauffeurs and changed the subject.

Cameron's voice and warm breath tickled her ear, and she jumped guiltily at the double stimuli.

"Is this your daily constitutional, or are you planning on leaving me stranded?"

When she halted to confront him, Cameron added with mock humility. "You wouldn't be that cruel? After all, I did behave like a gentleman tonight and virtuously forbore asking for a reward."

Throwing him a withering glance, she warned, "Don't press your luck. The night's not over yet."

As she reached her car, Cameron was at her elbow. "I was hoping you'd say that," he murmured.

She shook her head and breathed in disbelief, "You're incredible. Absolutely and utterly incredible."

"Allow me to prove it to you," he offered.

Halina stared for a stunned moment, reading the gleam in his gaze, and felt a shiver of anticipation course through her in response to the male message in the green eyes.

"No, thank you," she answered with less firmness than she'd intended. Hoping to cover her weak denial, she said, "And you ought to be careful not to offend the driver. There's a marked difference between taking the el at night and going home in the comfort of a chauffeured car."

"And you think I'd sacrifice my principles for the sake of self-interest?" he mocked, taking a step so that his body sandwiched hers against the car. "Besides, there's always taxis."

She ignored the flames shooting to the rest of her body from their point of contact and answered somewhat unsteadily, "You're welcome to try to flag one down."

He shook his head solemnly, his body resting more fully against hers. "My mother taught me to always go home with my escort." He smiled at her squirming efforts, and Halina stopped abruptly as she became cognizant of the effect they were having on him. "Guess you're stuck with me."

Opting for a reasonable approach that would blunt Cameron's wicked teasing, she asked with weary patience, "Don't you think it's time we started home?"

"Oh, I don't know. I feel quite comfortable right now," he said infuriatingly, shifting his body so that it wouldn't press her uncomfortably against the car and placing his arm around her back to bring her closer into the saddle of his thighs.

Her eyes brightened as she remembered his promise, and she said smugly, "But you said I was to decide when the evening is over. And I say now."

His eyes narrowed speculatively. He'd obviously forgotten his promise in the heat of the moment—and it was suddenly torrid, she decided, wiping drops of perspiration from her upper lip with the tip of her tongue.

It was quite apparent that he didn't want to give in, but there was no way out for him unless he broke his promise. And Halina intuitively knew Cameron was a man of his word, despite his teasing and unabashed male appetite.

He reluctantly moved his body from hers and said dryly, "You're certainly a worthy opponent. I'll have to give you that."

"Opponent? I wasn't aware we were at war," she lied smoothly, releasing her suppressed breath in a rush.

"Not at war, but in conflict," he qualified as she turned and opened both doors simultaneously with the master lock in the driver's door. Cameron helped her get seated before going on to the passenger side and gave her a lazy grin as he agilely contorted his large frame onto the seat. "But there's no possible doubt of the outcome," he added with maddening confidence.

Pressing her lips together, Halina bit back an answer and concentrated on her driving. She curved her way down the spiraling exit with a lot more speed than usual, the tires screeching under the unaccustomed abuse, hoping to shake him out of his male complacency. But Cameron merely rearranged his long legs, stretching them as far as he could into the available space, and added to her frustration by saying in sincere praise, "On top of it all, the lady is a terrific driver."

Halina joined the traffic on Michigan Avenue and shortly turned into Lake Shore Drive, keeping in the slow lane so that she could enjoy the view of the lakefront.

Sliding down in the seat another inch, Cameron put his head back and, linking his hands over his taut flat stomach, told her thickly, "Wake me when we're home."

Chapter

6

HALINA TURNED INTO the alley by her building and parked in the spot bearing her name on the concrete divider. Studying the man sleeping next to her, uncomfortably sprawled in the cramped interior, she felt a wave of tenderness as she saw how the thick black hair curled damply on the wide forehead and how, in repose, he looked far younger than his thirty-two years. His shoulder was braced against hers and his left hand rested on her thigh. It scorched her skin with surprising intensity now that part of her mind was not concentrated on driving, or admiring the beauty that was Lake Michigan on a starry summer night.

Moving her hand to take his off her lap, she smiled as she remembered how quickly he had fallen asleep, despite her hellish descent along the parking lot ramp and her racing entry onto the expressway. While it said a lot about his confidence in her driving, it certainly didn't say much for the effect of her company on him.

Shaking her head at the perversity of her inconsistency—not wanting this man to pursue her, yet growing piqued if he fell asleep next to her—she finally forced her hovering hand to descend on the one gently gripping the smooth firm muscles of her thigh, removing it from her sensitized flesh.

Her action seemed to nudge him into wakefulness, but Halina didn't release his hand because she noticed suddenly that it was burningly hot—and obviously not from the same heat that was assailing her.

As he lifted his head with obvious effort, a beam of light fell on his flushed face and Halina saw that his eyes were glazed. She now understood why his straight hair was clinging to his head in tight waves. Cameron was burning with fever. He seemed to be trying to focus his eyes on her; through what appeared to be a supreme exertion of willpower, he forced a smile onto his firm lips, their sensual curve not yielding their usual charm, distorted in a grimace of pain.

His brain was not affected, though, because he looked at his hand still held in hers, and the feverish gleam seemed to intensify.

"How nice to wake from a dream and find out it's continuing into reality," he said huskily.

When Halina tried to let go of his hand, intending to explain the situation, he turned his wrist so that he was grabbing her strong slender fingers. Cameron placed her hand over his heart, which was racing with the speed she'd hoped to induce earlier with her driving maneuvers. Another sign that Cameron was not well.

"I'm all yours," he said against her mouth, his chest alarmingly moist under the thin shirt.

Halina tried to pull away, irritation now mingling with her concern. "Listen, you're burning up—"

"You know I am," he interjected smoothly, his sexy whisper doing crazy things to her own pulse rate. "Ever since the first day I saw you. You'll just have to put me out of my misery."

"Oh, I intend to," Halina told him caustically, when another attempt at extricating herself failed. "If you don't let go of my hand soon, I'll have to borrow a tranquilizer gun from a vet friend of mine."

"And I had you pegged as the kind-to-animals type," he murmured amusedly, but his voice was getting weaker and his grip slackened.

Taking advantage of it, Halina pulled her hand away and took the keys from the ignition. "That just shows you how wrong first impressions can be."

She heard his chuckle as he opened his door, and she quickly hurried to the passenger side to give him the support she knew he'd need.

Cameron struggled his long frame out of the car and stood somewhat unsteadily, laughter filling his voice as he said, "Hey, you didn't have to get me drunk. I was perfectly willing."

"You fool." She grabbed his arm and wound it around her shoulders, supporting his weight as she began leading him into the house.

"I'll have to try this more often. Reversal of roles has some side benefits I'd never anticipated."

Halina ground her teeth, needing all her energy to support the big man.

"Hey, you're short, aren't you?" he said with the air of a man making an earth-shattering discovery.

Shaking off his arm, she rounded on him. "You're the absolute end. I should just let you . . ."

Cameron interrupted her weakly, "No insult intended," he slurred. "You're always so condemning and threatening, you seem six feet tall."

"Me, threatening?" Fixing him with an icy stare, she told him, "You're lucky you're—disabled right now. Otherwise I'd floor you."

Wordlessly Halina put her arm around his waist again and his arm around her shoulder. She noticed the effort he made to take most of his weight off her and to control the shakes that tore through his body. But as she braced him against the wall for a moment while she opened the back door, he still had enough presence of mind to quip, "My very own Florence Nightingale," which earned him another irate rebuke.

The seemingly never-ending trek to his bedroom had Halina's dress clinging to her from the combined moistness of his skin and hers. Even in this situation, with her flesh hot and damp from her efforts and from their enforced closeness, the man still seemed to be reaching out to her with sensual tentacles.

As soon as she had Cameron inside the room and safely installed on the bed, which she noticed was the one the previous tenants had left, she went to the phone. Cameron, rousing himself from his stupor, whispered, "What are you doing?"

"Calling you a doctor, what else?"

"No!" Cameron told her in an unsteady voice, "Don't need one. Just some rest."

Halina looked at him, doubt and concern on her soft features, and read the inflexibility in his eyes. Putting down the phone, she went to his side, and Cameron collapsed once more on the bed.

His eyes opened again as he felt the bed sink under her weight when she sat. "I've been meaning to get some new furniture, but haven't found the time." Halina leaned over him to help him take off his jacket, and noticed with renewed ire that he was again resting against her, letting her slender body support his hard weight. "This bed isn't good for much, unless you like the accompaniment of squeaky springs as a sound effect when making love."

"You mean having sex, don't you?" she asked acidly, giving him a shove that had him lying back on the bed.

"There's a difference?" he asked innocently, his lips curved in a slight smile that displayed their sensual fullness.

"If you have to ask . . ." she retorted, pulling his shirt out of his pants and then sliding it down his muscular chest so she could unbutton it.

The answer he was about to give died on his lips as shudders began racking his body once more, and with the last of his strength Cameron helped Halina remove his shirt and pants.

Concerned as she was about Cameron's health—and unsure whether she was doing the right thing in not calling a doctor—Halina was still affected by the leashed power and muscular symmetry of his body. His scar, wide and raw, seemed merely to emphasize his masculinity.

Halina decided to leave his black briefs on. She forcibly tore her gaze from his virile beauty and covered him quickly, tucking the bedclothes about him firmly when he tried to throw them off, hot as he was with fever.

From the closet she got another blanket, tucking it about him carefully so he couldn't get his arms out. She coaxed him to swallow two aspirin. Then she went to the bathroom and soaked several towels in cold water.

When the fever wouldn't break after an hour of soakings, Halina left him for a few moments to get some sheets and more ice cubes. She then helped him up and into a chair and changed the drenched sheets.

As she was helping him back to bed, Cameron put his hands on her shoulders, swaying on unsteady feet, and said hoarsely, "Wait...I need to get out of these damn shorts. They're sticking to my skin."

Gritting her teeth, Halina leaned him against the nearest wall and complied with his request, sliding the shorts down the long rock-hard thighs. She bit back a few epithets on bikini briefs and on men in general when the material clung to his skin like glue, and did her best to keep her head averted.

But her face must have been visible in the dim glow of the bedside lamp, because Cameron whispered tauntingly, "The color pink becomes you."

"Damn you! Can't you even behave when you're sick?"

He chuckled weakly. "I'd have to be dead not to appreciate your company, even if it is somewhat unwilling."

"I'm surprised you've lived this long," she muttered as she helped him back into bed.

"I plan to be around for a long time. I just overdid it

tonight, that's all," he murmured.

Looking at her as she covered him up and none too gently put another towel filled with ice cubes on his forehead, he winced and said, "You sure make a lousy nurse. Your bedside manner is terrible."

"I'm sure yours is above reproach," she told him sweetly. Noticing how his eyelids started to close, she asked with some alarm, "Are you sure you don't want a doctor? I could—"

He shook his head. "No. I'll be okay after a few hours of rest. I've been in a car accident and my doctor told me to take it easy..." He opened his eyes again, fixing her with his keen green gaze, and said ruefully, "Stupid of me. Look at the chance I had, and I had to overdo it..."

The slurring of his words was pronounced, and he again fell into a restless sleep. Halina kept him covered and continued replacing the ice packs, hoping her limited medical knowledge would suffice.

After a couple of hours of steady struggles with Cameron, the covers, and the ice, Halina breathed easier when the fever broke and he fell into a deeper sleep. Pulling a chair closer to the bed, she propped her legs on the mattress and eased her exhausted body into the sharp angles of the chair, the tension leaving her gradually before she too fell asleep.

Halina emerged from her sleep as if drugged, her body waking by degrees as she noticed that daylight was flooding the room. She rubbed her stiff neck wearily, turning it from side to side, wincing at the pain that resulted.

She moved her numb legs from the edge of the bed and memories of last night invaded her mind. At the same time awareness of where she was hit her and she had the sensation of being watched.

Her head snapped sideways and she saw Cameron Connors looking at her with gleaming eyes—only this time the glitter of his gaze was not caused by the fever.

She got up self-consciously, knowing she must look a wreck, her dress as crumpled and misshapen as she felt her body must be after sleeping on the uncomfortable wooden chair.

But concern over her appearance disappeared instantly when she saw that Cameron, although still pale under his golden-brown tan, was looking a lot better.

She picked up the wet towel lying on the floor and sat on the edge of the bed. Checking his forehead, she found it was now cool, though covered by a light film of perspiration.

"Well, it seems you'll live after all," she said dryly, to cover the odd rush of relief flooding through her.

She tried to remove her hand and gather her composure, but was unable to do either because Cameron claimed her hand, pressing it against his chest. "Don't go, please," he asked huskily. "I really feel something funny right here."

"Probably hunger pangs," Halina retorted, attempting to retrieve her fingers.

But Cameron had obviously recuperated during the past few hours because he pulled on her wrist with a graceful, easy show of force, toppling her onto him.

Her lips parted in surprise and protest, and he took advantage by invading her honeyed moistness, his tongue caressing the insides of her lips and the sweet barrier of her teeth before completing his plunder and engaging hers with rough sensuality.

Halina instinctively withdrew, trying to retreat within herself at this new crack in her defensive wall. But he said softly into her ear, "Don't. Don't close yourself up to me." When he moved her to one side to throw off the covers and mold her to him, Halina began to experience the long-forgotten delight of a male body imprinted on her soft curves.

As Cameron brought her even more fully into contact

with him, Halina murmured unsteadily, "I think I liked you better a while ago, when you were manageable."

His rich throaty chuckle made his tall frame vibrate against her. "And I liked you better on the dance floor, when you finally let go and turned soft in my arms."

Although Halina tried to trap the deep pulsation of need that rose unbidden from her very core, she found it impossible to do so when Cameron's obvious appreciation of her—his tactile exploration stimulating her through the material of her dress—joined his whispered encouragement in combustible combination.

His caresses were slow and languorous, his passion-roughened words erotic. When Cameron started to undress her, Halina found that all her objections and reservations dissolved like the first snowflakes on spring-warmed ground, and her enjoyment of the evening with him, her worry over his health, and his reawakening of her dormant desires merged into an overwhelming urge to experience his possession.

Halina returned his caresses with feverish intensity, gratified to hear his ragged breathing, pressing her heated flesh against his velvet-smooth muscularity in an effort to assuage the empty ache of her loins. Her dress was pushed aside in the scorching need of the moment, and was soon followed by her satin bra and panties.

But when Cameron covered her body with his and gently parted her trembling thighs, the past reared its cold dousing head. The old distrust of men, lurking in the shadows, snaked its way back into the present, and in the moment of possession her body arched in remembered fear. Cameron, lost in an ecstatic haze, mistook her convulsive movement for sensual encouragement and took her, holding her body tightly to his.

There was no pain, but neither was her passion sated. Coldness and loneliness replaced the warm, giving feelings of a few minutes past, and her body assumed an unnatural stillness.

As if sensing her mental withdrawal, Cameron leaned on his elbow and looked down at her, his eyes a warm green as he brushed wet tendrils of her red-brown hair away from her flushed face.

"You were right about the hunger pangs. And you certainly appeased my appetite."

Although his tone was gently teasing, Halina avoided his frank, still-hungry look, thinking bitterly that it was typical of a male to consider his needs first. Her body was cold, her mind seething with anger and frustration. Why she was so hurt—since Cameron had certainly not forced her, nor had the experience been totally unpleasant—she didn't want to delve into.

But when she tried to rise and put some protective distance between them, Cameron pushed her back gently.

"What's wrong?"

Halina faced him angrily, ready to hate him. She wanted to place the blame on him for everything. For her giving in and for her being disappointed—just as she had known she would be. She ignored the fact that she'd been fighting the pull of his attraction, as well as the gradual revival of her desires, since she'd first laid eyes on him, and that the evening in his company had solidified that reluctant attraction.

Although she tried to camouflage her hurt vulnerability with anger, he cupped her chin in his long steady fingers and asked softly, "You didn't enjoy it, did you?"

Halina felt the backs of her eyes burning. He was digging too deep and she was afraid to open up, afraid he would destroy all her carefully built defenses.

She tried to get away once more, not wanting to disgrace herself by crying. His gentleness and genuine interest were too hard to take.

But Cameron trapped her body with his, apparently not regarding her tears as the manipulative ploy Jeffrey had. His gaze intensifying, Cameron said in a voice husky with renewed desire, "I know I was at fault. I was too aroused and lost control too soon. I usually do notice whether I'm satisfying a woman."

Halina blushed at his easy assumption of guilt, and at the unaffected honesty and directness of his words.

"I apologize. I know the first time between two lovers can often be awkward but, toward the end of the evening we seemed to be so attuned to one another's feelings." Running a finger in a straight line from the tip of her nose down her chin and throat, he added throatily, "So please let me try again. I wouldn't want to leave a customer unsatisfied."

Cameron Connors was an infuriating puzzzle: On the one hand, he didn't consider her lack of satisfaction her own failing, but rather his; on the other, his reference to her as a "customer," however jesting, was not something she found amusing. And, as for her feelings, what did he really know about her or her past? What did she really know about him? There were too many unanswered questions between them. But she wasn't about to bare her soul to him—especially not at this moment. Yet she had to say something.

"Men don't care if they provide satisfaction. They're only interested in getting it," she said coldly. "I'm sure your offer has nothing to do with my own gratification— you're merely after a repetition of your own."

The change in Cameron's expression would have been comical had she been in the mood to laugh. As it was, his surprise allowed her to slip out of his loosened hold, and she picked up his discarded robe from the foot of his bed en route to the door.

From the corner of her eye she saw her dress and underthings in an intimate pile on the floor as she flew past, but was deterred from returning to pick them up when she heard the rusty squeak of bedsprings behind her. She quickly opened the door, guessing that not even Cameron Connors would follow her into the hall in his birthday suit. There were too many older people in the building who would certainly be shocked if they saw him.

She was right. Cameron stopped in his tracks, frustration crossing his handsome features as she left his apartment and stood just outside, after carefully checking the hall and belting his black robe securely about her slender waist. Whichever course he took—whether he tried to grab another robe from the closet a few feet away, or make a grab for her—would be unsuccessful.

Halina smiled at his dilemma. Her anger and pain receded as she began to appreciate the potential of the situation. For once *she* was in control. She looked him up and down across the length of the living room, enjoying the virile view he presented as he stood framed in the bedroom doorway. His long legs were braced far apart in disgusted helplessness, his powerful bronzed torso rippling with wiry muscles, the angry red scar—which now seemed another usual detail in the intoxicating whole—highlighting his masculine symmetry as it ran diagonally from a point at the side of his chest to a spot right above his groin.

Her attention wandered as she noticed how his body began to respond to her appreciative, openly inspecting gaze.

"You little vixen. Doing this to me when I can't do anything about it."

Halina raised her eyes to his face, knowing she dared not prolong this moment, since Barkley Court would be stirring in a few minutes. It wouldn't do for the landlady to be found outside the new young tenant's apartment in his robe.

"Are you going to allow me a chance to redeem myself?"

His request, uttered in an appealingly seductive voice, startled her out of her delicious reflections and her visual feast. He was willing to assume the blame for something that was mostly her fault. Perhaps if she told him about Jeff...

No! Her mind screamed in denial, pushing down her tentative new feelings. She couldn't take the chance. It had been a painful, humiliating fiasco with Jeff. And although this time there hadn't been the physical pain that had accompanied her loss of virginity, the humiliation and doubts—also present in her experience with Louis—were all too real now.

Cameron took a step forward. "Talk to me, Halina. What's the matter?"

But she merely shook her head and, turning sharply, ran to her apartment as if the hounds of hell were after her. She took the spare key from its hiding place and unlocked the door with shaking fingers. She heard Cameron call her, but ignored the entreaty in his voice.

Halina locked the door, knowing he would come after her. She knew he had the right to an explanation. But she couldn't face him right now. The doorknob rattled, and she took a deep breath to calm herself.

"Open up, Halina. We have to talk."

"Please go away. You're going to wake up everyone in the building."

"So open up—or everyone *will* see me pounding on your door."

Halina whispered brokenly, "I can't." She put her hands over her ears to muffle Cameron's low-voiced arguments and his heated accusation that she was acting as if he'd attempted rape.

Resisting the urge to fling open the door, she asked him quietly to go away. She could sense the struggle on the other side of the door, and after a few charged moments, he was gone.

She moved defeatedly toward the bathroom, wondering if Cameron had given up because he thought it best to talk at another time, when their emotions weren't running so high. Or, had he decided she just wasn't worth the chase? As she washed her face with cold water, then brushed her chestnut hair, Halina tried to convince herself that the latter choice would be better all around.

Chapter

7

TWO WEEKS LATER, as Halina was leaving her apartment on a Friday morning, she saw Cameron walking rapidly down the hall. He was dressed in a pin-striped business suit and carried a leather attaché case.

She didn't call out to him and was glad he didn't notice her. Cameron had tried to speak to her a couple of times since the morning she'd gone to bed with him. But she had made it clear she didn't want to discuss it. He had said he'd leave her alone for the moment, but they would talk things over eventually.

Halina had found her thoughts straying often to Cameron during the interim. In a way, she was glad he had appeared at a moment in her life when she'd needed distraction from her loss. She had loved her father very much and had tried hard to please him—perhaps because of his indifference.

Halina had never stopped missing the warm, nurturing childhood days. Her mother and grandparents had showered her with love, and had instilled in her a respect for learning, hard work, independence. But those rich, trusting relationships had been ruptured with her mother's death—and the sudden withdrawal of her father's love when she'd needed it the most had demoralized and confused her for a while. Gradually she had made the best of the situation by seeing to her father's comfort and acting as his companion when he was not busy with some experiment. But life with her father was incomplete. And she had looked elsewhere, putting her faith and trust in

81

another man, who had carelessly betrayed her.

But Cameron was unlike any man she knew, and Halina found that her rare spare time, and even her working hours, were invaded with thoughts of him.

She was puzzled by his activities. She'd seen him leave several times early in the morning, dressed in a business suit. But there didn't seem to be any regularity to his hours. And Halina couldn't very well ask him, when she herself had refused to discuss other matters with him.

Although it went against her grain, she had casually managed to bring the subject up with some of her tenants, but no one knew what Cameron did for a living. And Halina found to her chagrin that she was not overjoyed at having a man of mystery in her building. Especially, she thought, smiling wryly as she got into her car and left Barkley Court, when she still didn't know what the mystery was after weeks of wondering.

Her counseling sessions with a freshman who had decided to change her major from education to computer science, and a premed senior who didn't think he would make it as a doctor and wanted to enter dental school in the fall, kept her mind off Cameron. But as she drove back later that day, she found that her thoughts had once again turned to her intriguing tenant.

As she pulled into the Barkley Court parking lot, she saw Cameron, in disreputable cutoffs and an even sadder T-shirt, washing Mrs. Tate's car.

Mrs. Tate was the oldest tenant, a spry eighty-three-year-old woman whose husband had died two years ago. Although she seldom drove, she still kept her husband's brown Ford. She couldn't part with it, she'd told Halina repeatedly, and she washed it faithfully every week as a labor of love.

Halina got out of her car, making every effort to keep her eyes away from the thighs that gleamed with healthy perspiration and the tight male buttocks that strained under the worn material as Cameron expertly applied wax to the car.

"Need your car washed?" He grinned at her, his glance direct and appreciative in the quick but thorough look that took in her dark-brown skirt and coral blouse.

Looking at her dirty two-door, Halina had to admit that it could use a wash.

Perversely she told him, "I could always take it to the gas station."

"Oh, come on!" Cameron chided. "That's the lazy way out. You know they don't do as good a job as a proud owner would. That's assembly-line work, and they can only get cars superficially clean—especially when there's a long line."

"And I suppose you have *always* washed and waxed your own car," she asked pointedly, curious to know about his background and his past and present jobs.

"Well...not always," he admitted sheepishly. "But I'm finding out just what I've been missing."

Halina had hoped her dig might make him disclose the reason he had no car of his own. She didn't know the details of his accident, but she didn't think Cameron was afraid of anything. He'd certainly demonstrated no fear during his ride in her car.

His chuckle told her he was taking her honeyed hostility in stride, and that he wasn't about to satisfy her curiosity. Halina felt uneasy. She really had no right to question him. He hadn't done anything wrong—unless she could find some way of blaming him for the fact that she was finding it increasingly harder to resist him. Where was her famed immunity to men now that she really needed it?

"All right. I might consider having my car washed by an expert. But what will it cost me?"

"Ah, so the lady doesn't trust an innocent, neighborly offer." Cameron grinned and fixed her with a stare that started the sexual tension crackling between them.

"You're right, the lady doesn't believe in freebies," she retorted swiftly. "And," she added for good measure, "nothing remotely associated with you could ever be considered innocent."

"Ouch!" He pantomimed a hit. Putting the finishing touches on the Ford, now all shiny paint, chrome, and glass, he suggested blithely, "Tell you what. How about you taking *me* out to dinner this time?"

"At loose ends again?" she asked wryly.

He cleaned his hands on a paper towel and came to stand in front of her, his musky scent, enhanced by sunwarmed perspiration, attacking her susceptible senses. Putting one hand on the roof of the car, he leaned closer to her and murmured huskily, "You have to admit I'm effective. I think you were able to forget about your father for a little while."

More than a little while, she thought. "Yes, you were certainly effective. But I'm a big girl now, and I think your methods of helping one to forget cause more trouble than they remedy." Trying for a lighter note, she said, "As to your offer, I think I'll pass. I can get my car washed for a couple of dollars. Buying you dinner seems a bit extreme."

"How about if I throw in an oil change and general checkup?" he offered magnanimously. "Not to say anything about my sparkling conversation, inimitable company..."

"Oh, you're inimitable, all right," Halina said deflatingly. "But I think our interpretations of your uniqueness would differ drastically." She changed her heavy briefcase from her right hand to her left and asked him dubiously, "Besides, are you sure you know anything about cars?"

"Your confidence in me is overwhelming," Cameron said dryly. "Here, let me take your case." He did not step back to put more breathing space between them once he relieved her of her briefcase. He merely stood in front of her, smiling wickedly as Halina tried to take shallow breaths so that her breasts would not brush against his chest. When that didn't work, she subtly moved a few inches sideways, and Cameron allowed her the shift, settling himself against the car she was leaning on, though keeping his hip in burning contact with hers.

She crossed her arms over her breasts to hide the betraying thrust of her nipples against the silk blouse. Aiming for nonchalance and achieving only an odd half-strangled sound, she coughed delicately to cover her false start and said coolly, "You still didn't explain your supposed prowess."

"Oh, I only claim prowess in one area," he drawled. Halina's head swung sideways, but the sight of those laughing all-seeing eyes taking in her discomfort with supreme enjoyment had her facing straight ahead again. "In cars"—he paused infuriatingly—"I admit only competence."

"Bully for you," she shot back, sidestepping his first comment as if it were an active mine field. "And where did you acquire your competence?"

"I worked as a mechanic to pay for graduate school."

A golden opportunity! "And what was it you studied in college?" she asked casually.

He set her briefcase on the car's black hood and snaked an arm to trap her against the door. Bending his black head, he whispered in her ear, "I'll show you tonight what I learned in college."

Halina put her hand on his forearm, intending to remove it from her body. When her palm came in contact with the rock-solid flesh, she forgot her purpose momentarily. But her fingers stopped their automatic caressing of the vital male body when his right hand came up to cover hers gently.

Pivoting, she grabbed the briefcase with one hand and knocked his arm off with the other. Cameron made no move to stop her.

"Does that mean no?" he asked wryly. "You're really missing out on the benefits of my expertise." At her raised eyebrows, he added, "With the car."

"If it'll make you happy," she said with an indifferent shrug as she headed for the back entrance, "by all means get at it."

"What time do I pick you up tonight?" he asked as she reached the door.

Halina let her hand drop slowly from the doorknob and turned reluctantly. "You never give up, do you?"

Cameron shook his head and Halina noticed with resentful pleasure how the rays of the afternoon sun haloed the black head with blue highlights.

"Another one of my virtues. Boundless determination."

"More like a bad case of hardheadedness," she muttered. Thinking fast, she came up with the perfect solution.

"I don't think I like the look in your eyes," he said lazily, straightening his long body from the car.

Halina smiled sweetly and said, "You can pick me up tomorrow. We'll leave bright and early for a picnic at Lake Villa."

"A picnic!" She could hear the unuttered groan in Cameron's voice, and she gloated. Brightening, he asked hopefully, "A secluded picnic, with you, me, and the sun and the trees . . ."

"And a few hundred other people," she finished cheerfully. "You don't have to worry about providing the food—"

"That's the least of my worries."

"We can eat there. There'll be German food, as well as entertainment. And I'll knock on your door at seven o'clock."

The dismay on his face almost had her skipping, happy at having disconcerted *him* for once. Halina was heading for the door when his voice wafted quietly to her. "Not so fast."

Turning once more, Halina kept her face expressionless. "Yes?"

"You have to help. Wash or wax. Take your pick."

His shark smile started her blood boiling. "You said *you'd* be doing it."

"I never said I'd do it alone. Besides, I have to check your engine. You wouldn't want me to overexert myself, would you?"

Briefcase heavy in her hand, blouse clinging to her moist skin, Halina bit out slowly, "From personal experience, I'd say I rather prefer you prone."

As soon as the words left her mouth, Halina wanted to recall them.

"Didn't I say we had a lot in common? I also like you horizontal."

"You know that's not what I meant," she snapped.

"Or is it that you enjoyed nursing me? As I remember, your bedside manner improved vastly—"

Mrs. Tate chose that moment to come through the door, nearly knocking Halina off her feet.

"Oh, I'm sorry, dear. Did I hurt you?"

"No, no. It's all right. It was careless of me to stand in front of the door like that," Halina said quickly, breathing deeply to restore some air to her abused lungs.

"And how are you doing, Halina?" she asked, the bright blue eyes sharp and curious as they darted shrewdly between Halina and Cameron. "Isn't Cameron just a darling? What a delightful, helpful young man."

"Oh, he sure is," Halina said through clenched teeth, giving Cameron a killing glance. "If you'll excuse me, I have some things to attend to . . ."

"I'll be waiting, Halina," Cameron called cheerfully.

As she stepped into the building, Halina heard Mrs. Tate asking, "Is Halina going to be joining you? You know, Cameron, Halina is a lovely, hardworking girl . . ."

The words were still ringing in her ears as Halina slammed the door shut after her and walked down the hallway to her apartment.

When she emerged from the building a few minutes later, Halina saw that Cameron had filled a pail with water and had again readied the hose.

"Men's clothing sure does a lot more for you than it does for me," Cameron drawled, his gaze taking in the faded jeans that clung to her hips and derriere, and an old shirt she'd knotted under her bust, exposing a band of ivory skin at her waist.

Shaking her head in pure frustration, Halina demanded, "Doesn't your mind entertain any other thoughts?"

"With you around? I'd have to be—"

"Dead," Halina finished for him in disgust.

"See? I told you I'd grow on you," Cameron told her cheerfully, whistling tonelessly as he handed her a rag. "You're already reading my mind."

"Not quite," she retorted dryly. "Or I wouldn't be around right now." As she poured soap onto the rag, she added casually, "But I'll have to admit—we do have *one* thing in common."

Cameron turned eagerly toward her, leaning his elbows on the hood of her car. "And that is?" he asked expectantly.

"You can carry a tune about as well as I can," she said innocently. And ducked quickly as a pailful of water came sailing her way.

Throwing herself forward, she tucked her head and rolled toward the hose, reaching it a fraction of a second before Cameron, who had divined her intention. She aimed it at him and let loose a strong torrent that hit Cameron squarely in the face.

He gasped and choked on a mouthful of water, but

before she could get him a second time, he'd disappeared on the other side of her car.

Halina backed up warily, closing off the nozzle, but ready to open it again at the first sight of Cameron.

She saw a white cloth rise slowly from behind the car, and she laughed. "Ready to surrender?"

Cameron's head cautiously followed. He waited a minute to see whether she'd attack again, but when Halina kept the hose pointing downward, he rose to his full height. "The Connorses have never surrendered. Called a truce, maybe. Surrendered, no."

"How about a cowardly retreat?"

"Calling a Connors a coward? That deserves punishment, woman," he growled, beginning to walk around the car.

Halina raised the huge hose menacingly and Cameron halted in his tracks. "On the other hand, I've always thought timing was everything," he added judiciously, picking up a couple of tools and opening the hood to examine the engine.

Halina laughed again, and was surprised at how relaxed she felt in his company all of a sudden. But she didn't let down her guard. Pleasant and fun Cameron could be. But trustworthy, that was another matter.

They worked in happy camaraderie for the next half hour. But as she polished the last bit of chrome on the inside of the car and snapped the door shut, Halina felt her skin tingling—and it was not from the heat.

She raised her head, sensing a presence the way a deer in the forest does, and encountered Cameron's smoldering gaze on her. It trapped her, and she could only look on helplessly as he came slowly toward her, as if he knew a sudden movement might break the spell.

"Do you know the effect you have on me?" he asked in a hoarse voice as he stopped next to her and grabbed the long loose braid that hung down her back, bringing it over to rest on one breast. His fingers retained possession of the braid, his hand branding the upper swell of her flesh through the double covering of shirt and bra.

"With those curves, that face, and this hair, you are one dangerous piece of femininity."

"That's partly what I object to," Halina told him earnestly, her hand coming up to grab his as she tried to make him understand. Jeff and practically every other man she'd met had made her feel like an object. There had been a point when she'd actually wished she were plain looking. But not anymore. Now she figured she was what she was—and the rest was the man's problem.

But it was somehow important that Cameron understand.

"You've just referred to me as a piece. Men too often do see women as a piece of . . . a side of beef," she ended lamely.

He raised his head slowly at her statement. "Lady, you're wrong. There are men out there who might see all women as commodities. But not all of them, and certainly not me. And certainly not with you. It isn't just your body, but your—"

"But your mind," she finished bitterly, curiously disappointed. She'd heard that line countless times, and Cameron seemed much too sophisticated and experienced to resort to that type of verbal play.

He tugged gently on her braid, bringing her attention back to him. "Not polite to interrupt," he chided gently. "I wonder why you're so ready to think the worst of me."

His perceptive comment battered her severely breached defenses, and she desperately tried to shore them up again. She tried to pry his fingers loose from her hair and push her way past him, into the relative safety of her building. But his free hand curved around her waist and brought her body into contact with his hip, his fingers wrapping about her braid in a tight hold.

Afraid of what he might say, afraid he might already

guess she was halfway in love with him, Halina said scathingly, "I see. You want to get back at me for that episode in your apartment, for teasing you. You know, instead of trying to pay me back for saying no the second time you wanted to have sex, you might have thanked me for taking care of you."

For one tense moment she thought she'd been successful. His body hardened at her words and his eyes narrowed. But she knew she'd lost when he forced his body to relax and, releasing her braid, lifted his hand to gently caress her neck.

"First of all, I didn't have sex with you—I made love to you. Second, I hadn't pegged you for the type who asked for thanks afterward." Her cheeks grew warm. He had twisted her words around, and he knew it. "But since you have, then let me tell you I appreciated your noble sacrifice and would have told you so had you given me the opportunity. But then, you didn't stick around for thanks. Nor anything else. Why?"

"No doubt you'll tell me. You seem to be writing the script as you go along," she said with cold anger, hating him for backing her into a corner.

Ignoring her words, he kneaded the flesh at her waist in a lazy, insidious pattern, forcing her to relax.

Her voice cracked as she demanded, "Please take your hands off me. I resent being made to listen, or seduced into compliance. Since women can't physically force men into hearing everything they have to say, I think you're taking unfair advantage."

His fingers dug into her hip and for a moment she knew he wanted to shake her. Brute strength was one male prerogative she'd never considered fair at all, though it was something she was prepared for. If he let go of her hair and gripped her by the shoulders, he'd find himself with a very painful knee jab.

Halina could almost sympathize with him. Men were

raised to go after what they wanted, to take it by force
if necessary. But a stronger man held back, kept himself
from using that same strength and power against someone
physically weaker.

"That's twice you've outmaneuvered me," he said at
length, dropping his hands from her body. "Three times
if you count your cute little baptism."

"Maybe you just needed your mouth washed out,"
Halina said somewhat unsteadily, her pulse slowing.

"I don't think so," he returned softly. "Regardless of
your suspicions, I happen to respect you—as well as
want you like hell."

Halina backed away from the force and conviction of
his words and let the rag drop from her hands. "Since
this was your idea, I'll let you do the cleanup. I have
some aptitude and personality tests to go through this
evening."

"I'll let you go this time," Cameron said, a subtle
warning in his voice. Halina wiped her palms on the seat
of her jeans and turned quickly away, before Cameron
could change his mind. As she got to the door, his voice
reached her.

"Halina?"

She turned back and was met by a stream of water.
Gasping from the shock, she put her hands up instinctively to shield herself, but Cameron was already turning
off the hose.

"Remember. I'll get you in the end. If it takes all four
months. Or more."

His last words returned to her mind over and over
during the night, and again in the morning, when she
was getting ready for the picnic.

She was tempted to cancel their date, but knew what
he'd make of that. She would have no pride in herself
if she turned coward.

Halina now realized that while she led a productive,

active life, she was not totally fulfilled. She had developed her academic potential, participated regularly in sports, was active in community affairs. But her personal life had grown sterile because, outside of Lorraine Morelli and her family—who had taken her into the bosom of their large warm clan—she had allowed no one else to get close. Her relationships with her tenants were casual and friendly, friendlier than in a lot of other apartment buildings. But she didn't confide her secret dreams to them, or her plans for the future.

As the cuckoo clock chimed the quarter hour, Halina jumped guiltily and hurriedly put on the terry knit romper she'd been fingering while lost in her reflections. The one-piece outfit could be tied halter style or worn strapless. She secured the pale-orange strap in front with a tight knot and smoothed the brief lemon shorts hugging her hips.

Looking at the alarm clock, Halina saw she had only ten minutes to finish getting ready. With the ease of long practice, she worked her hair into Italian braids and added an apricot ribbon that matched the stripes in the top half of the romper before a knock sounded on the hall door.

Her heart in her mouth, Halina took a deep breath and opened the door with what she hoped looked like cool composure, proud that the fingers that finished tying the ribbon did not tremble.

She mumbled good morning out of the corner of her mouth, her head bent over the braid she'd looped forward, and was surprised into stillness when Cameron gently tipped her chin up with a long forefinger and dropped a brief, hard kiss on her mouth.

Fighting down the stirrings of desire his single kiss had evoked, Halina told him, "I thought I was supposed to pick you up at your door this morning."

"After yesterday afternoon I wasn't sure the picnic was still on. Just making sure you didn't change your mind."

"You mean you're not sure of yourself with me? Even with your sparkling conversation, delightful company, good looks—"

"The only thing I'm sure of with you is that I can expect a lot of surprises," he interrupted her teasing tirade.

"Does that mean women have let you have your way all the time? How boring for you," she said, grinning. Her fingers played with her braid, which rested over one breast, and the look on his face told her he wanted to touch it, and perhaps continue on from there.

"Not boring. Restful." He sighed as he hooked his thumbs in the loops of his shorts, as if reminding himself to behave, to put his hands away before they began wandering. "What do you call that arrangement into which you've tortured your hair?"

"This?" she asked innocently, still toying with her braid. "It's an Italian braid, as opposed to a French braid. You just take the upper part of the hair and fix it into two small separate braids, and then you incorporate them into—"

"Quite interesting," he interjected politely, obviously not having expected a detailed explanation.

"You know, I've been trying to decide whether to have my hair cut. It's become such a bother, especially in sports..." She let her voice trail off, expecting him to be suitably horrified, as her father and Ted had been when she'd casually mentioned the idea to them.

His answer surprised her. "It would be a shame to cut such beautiful hair, but then, it wouldn't affect your attractiveness," he told her matter-of-factly. "With your looks, I'm sure you could have any number of hairdos and still be stunning. And I happen to like short hair on women. So if you care to oblige me, please do so."

Halina burst out laughing. She should have known Cameron would not fall for such a ploy.

"You have just settled the fate of my hair—at least

for the immediate future," she said as she picked up her small purse from the coffee table. "If you like short hair, then I'll leave mine long. Just as you wanted all along," she added as she caught the glint of humor in his eyes.

"Isn't it convenient that we understand each other so well?" he murmured as he opened the apartment door and let her precede him. "But you would really look beautiful in short hair—and absolutely nothing else," he added wickedly, almost causing her to drop the key before he took it from her to lock the door.

Chapter

8

"THAT WAS SWEET of you," Halina told Cameron as he jumped from the lowest branch of the tree after retrieving a soccer ball.

A group of girls and boys of ages six to eight had been playing soccer nearby, and when a husky boy had enthusiastically kicked the ball into the highest reaches of the tree, a little girl had enlisted Cameron's help.

Groaning at the appeal in the youngster's wide blue eyes, Cameron had, at Halina's urging, acceded. Glowering at Halina, he'd gamely climbed the large tree.

"Anything else you want me to accomplish today?" he asked with smooth sarcasm, rubbing his hands to remove some bark from his skin. "Climb the highest mountain, cross the largest ocean..."

"No, that should do it for the day," Halina said, trying to contain the quiver of her lips.

"You didn't tell me there'd be a cast of thousands here," Cameron said as a toddler ran smack into them, followed by a huge bounding dog of indeterminate breed watching over its tiny master. Cameron yanked Halina out of the way of the shaggy mammoth, and kept his hand around her waist. "Or that we'd be constantly dodging objects. This is worse than an obstacle course."

Halina turned her head away, trying to hide her laughter, but her shoulders shook and her mirth exploded. Cameron said softly, "I'm glad you consider this whole situation amusing."

"I—I'm sorry," Halina said between giggles. "But this

has certainly shown another side of your personality."

"Anything to oblige," Cameron muttered dryly. "But you'd better be careful with your pastry. It's in danger of collapsing."

Halina bit into the rich center, savoring her Mohn Strudel as they walked through the crowd at Lake Villa and Cameron steered them around a group of children dressed in dirndls and lederhosen.

Lunch had been delicious. They had chosen Wiener Schnitzel, and the breaded meat had been tender and spicy. Cameron had consumed two helpings of apple strudel and had suggested a walk after the big, satisfying meal.

He was being awfully good about everything, Halina had to admit, considering the fact that one of his first comments upon arriving had been that it looked as if they'd be knee-deep in people.

Throughout the morning they'd watched German groups perform native songs and dances, the colorful costumes and noisy enthusiasm more than making up for the lack of harmony or correct formation. Cameron had enjoyed both the food and the cultural offerings, but she knew he wasn't too happy about one aspect of the picnic. He had not had much luck in isolating her. Every time he'd maneuvered her close to him in what seemed a secluded spot, someone had inevitably appeared.

Besides the soccer team, there had been an elderly couple looking for their grandson, who, they had explained in delightful German-accented English, they were caring for that weekend so their daughter could take a second honeymoon with her husband. Cameron had barely recuperated from Halina's fifteen-minute talk with the couple when two girls had shown up with chocolates they were selling for a school fund raiser. Cameron had obligingly purchased half a dozen boxes (he'd later given them away to other children), answering Halina's raised eyebrows with, "If I buy that many, they will certainly remember. They won't approach us again."

But after traversing the whole picnic area looking for solitude, which was just not to be found, Cameron had apparently given up. Halina guessed he'd merely postponed his attack, waiting like a good strategist for a better opportunity.

She had to give him credit in one respect, though. Dozens of scantily clad beauties had come in and out of the grounds from the lake across the road, their young tanned bodies gleaming in their bikinis, but he'd still managed to concentrate on her. His single-minded attention flattered and pleased her, and it told her something of his willpower and determination. Watching another teenager, a knockout in a red string bikini, give him an openly encouraging look as she passed them on her way to the beach, Halina had to smile at the temptation the man was faced with. It must have been awfully hard on his hormones.

"What dastardly thoughts are lurking under that angelic smile?" he asked, startling her out of her reverie.

"Why, none, of course. Or I wouldn't be angelic, would I?" she answered ingenuously.

"Then why do I get the feeling that you're having a good laugh at my expense?" he asked ruefully.

"Maybe because I am," she confessed, her eyes roving his physique the way many of the girls' had.

He did look breathtakingly attractive, she decided. His brief white shorts emphasized the tanned muscularity of his legs, and his cobalt-blue shirt highlighted the thick raven hair and startling light eyes. She added with a self-mocking smile, "There seems to be some poetic justice in my bringing you to the picnic. You've certainly made a hit with the female half, and I suspect that some of the teenagers who have been eyeing you wouldn't mind taking you home with them."

"Hmmm," he said thoughtfully, stopping by a large tree and leaning against it as he folded his arms across his wide chest. "You know, there's a lot you've just revealed in that statement."

Halina fidgeted nervously at his side. "Really?" she asked with attempted insouciance.

He nodded, studying the tip of her nose, now pink from their hours in the sun. "You've just admitted you brought me here, which means you planned it. I wonder why." Giving her no chance to respond, he added, "I'm sure it was because you knew I would enjoy the German food and gemütlichkeit. But there's more to it, isn't there? You wanted to make sure I had no time alone with you." When she started to protest, he waved her words aside and said gently, "And you've certainly accomplished that. We might as well have gone downtown on Saint Patrick's Day. I'm sure the parade would have been less populated."

He smiled as he pulled her slowly toward him, fitting her body between the V of his parted legs. Halina found she liked his smile about as much as she did his hands: They both had a sure, knowing quality that made her bristle.

"And you certainly don't seem to mind that other women find me attractive." Halina stiffened within his hold and his hands went to her back, working a soothing pattern into her spine. "That, of course, is a refreshing change, as I'm tired of jealous, possessive women. You're not only a very secure lady in most areas, but you're also amazingly straightforward." He stopped his sensual rubbing and rested his hands on her hips, continuing to antagonize her with his cool analysis. "It could also indicate that you don't give a damn about me, and that would not be refreshing or satisfactory. But if you were totally indifferent to me, you certainly would not have felt forced to resort to a crowded picnic." His voice became as challenging as the pressure of his fingers on her flesh. "So which is it, Halina? Are you uninterested or too interested? And if the latter, why are you so scared?"

Pushing outward with her elbows and knocking his hands from her body, she stepped away from him and said in a trembling voice, "I'm not an object, do you understand? Nor am I an insect you can examine on a dissecting table."

"Why are you so afraid to take a good long look at yourself?"

"I have!" she fairly screamed. Then she quickly got herself under control. In a lower voice, she added feelingly, "But I'm not about to stand here and let you analyze me too. Jeff also felt it his divine right to point out—"

Horrified at what she'd been about to reveal, she clamped her mouth shut and prayed that he had missed her slip, or would at least ignore it.

But Cameron pounced on it. "Who's Jeff? Is he the one who's made you afraid of a man's touch? Who's made you doubt yourself—"

"Please stop," she requested wearily, torn between her need to confide in him and her fear of being disappointed again. "Jeff doesn't matter, and I don't want to discuss him." Seeing that he was going to pursue the subject, she asked quickly, bitterly, "I suppose you've taken a long, hard look at yourself?"

His expression tightened for a moment, a muscle jumping beneath the bronzed roughness of his jaw. "As a matter of fact," he said finally, "I have. And I know it takes a hell of a lot of pain and perseverance to get rid of the layers of defense and habits that human beings employ to erect a safe, comfortable existence for themselves."

"Next you're going to say we should all live in a monastery," she mocked, resentful of his words. "Or do monks also have something to hide?"

"No doubt," he returned calmly, his composure making tatters of her own. "But I think we're getting off the subject."

Walking blindly away from him, intent only on escaping his presistent digging, she threw over her shoulder, "I didn't know there was a subject. And I'm not under inspection."

He didn't answer, and she was grateful for the brief respite. She'd never met a man like Cameron before, and he scared her. He stimulated her intellectually as well as physically—unlike her usual dates, who showed little depth, talking only of their jobs and sports. But at least they were safe, predictable, and heeded her wishes— which was why she went out with them—while Cameron was totally unpredictable and enjoyed keeping her off balance.

"What did you mean when you said you'd taken a long look at yourself?" she couldn't help asking after a while.

When he didn't respond right away, she stole a look at him, and his grin told her he'd anticipated her question. Her normally placid nature became ruffled again, and she said huffily, "Forget it. It doesn't really matter, and *I* don't pry into other people's business."

As soon as the words left her mouth and she heard his husky chuckle, Halina wanted to take them back.

"You could have found out a lot if you hadn't insisted on avoiding me," he reminded her softly.

"Would you like to take a boat ride?" she asked with a wide innocent smile, deliberately switching subjects.

He laughed. "All right, we'll take a boat ride. But Halina," he added, putting a hand on her shoulder and turning her to face him, "we have to talk about it sometime. You can't keep running forever."

Halina looked into the warm green eyes, but couldn't hold his gaze. She felt a slow telltale flush steal up her cheeks and they began walking again, heading for the grassy parking lot where they'd left her car that morning.

Thirty minutes later they were seated in a small boat in a nearby lake, and Halina felt her back muscles screaming. It'd been a long time since she'd done any rowing, but she'd insisted on doing her share. Putting down the oars, she leaned back nonchalantly, trying to breathe evenly, and flashed Cameron what she hoped was a bright smile. She was afraid it was more like a grimace.

"Tired?" he asked solicitously, but Halina saw a grin quirking the corners of the finely sculpted male mouth.

She shook her head in casual denial. "No. I just thought we'd sit in the middle of the lake and take advantage of the sun," she said, lying through her teeth, since she'd never been able to tan. She merely boiled.

The sun was just then at its zenith, beating down unmercifully with iron-melting strength. Halina tried to take her mind off the heat and the black dots that were forming behind her eyes.

"How are you feeling?" She seemed to have taken him by surprise, and she asked again, "Are you feeling all right?"

"With you across from me on a small, unsteady boat? You've got to be kidding," he answered with self-mocking humor. "You really know how to pick them. First a teeming, albeit charming, picnic; now a small, although not so charming, boat. Very inspired."

"You said you'd taken a long look at yourself," she said softly, thinking of the women she'd seen him with, "but in one respect you've obviously not changed."

Seeing his bewilderment, she continued on a harsher note than she'd intended. He couldn't possibly know she'd seen him with those women. "The chase seems everything to you."

"If that were the case, then I'd be satisfied by now, wouldn't I?" At her startled look, he added harshly, "Make no mistake, sweetheart. Whether you got sufficient enjoyment out of the lovemaking that morning or not, I sure as hell did. And I've been waiting for you to be honest with yourself and admit you'd like to try again."

Halina tensed, instinctively rejecting his overture. She resented his unflagging efforts to make her face something she was not ready for—although, if she was honest, she'd have to admit that there would never be a proper time for it. She'd probably always find some rationalization to avoid further pain.

Even with the limited opportunities of the boat, Cameron was forcing her into awareness of him, his long legs making their own room on her seat as they rested comfortably against the firm flesh of her thighs.

Taking up the oars again, she began to propel the boat across the blue-green water, now rippling from the disturbance caused by some water-skiers. She told him in a low voice, "I'd rather not discuss it."

"All barriers up again, is that it?" he asked on a hard note, and Halina glanced up at him, surprised at the impatience in his tone. "You can't hide forever, and it's not as if we're total strangers."

"I'd have to trust you to confide in you," she told him bitterly, "and I don't think you've given me much cause to."

Cameron, about to speak, shook his head in weary resignation and sighed. He settled back in his seat, but Halina noted with infuriated impotence that he did not withdraw body contact. He remained in a lazy sprawl, his weight resting on his elbows, his legs firmly braced against hers.

Halina kept rowing absently, lost in contemplation, until she became aware of a certain restlessness on Cameron's part. He had previously remained quiet, except for his well-placed rubbing and brushes against her flesh, but he was now literally rocking the boat. Frowning, she gave him the severe look she reserved for her brilliant students who got *D*'s in her classes because of laziness or hell raising.

Noticing Cameron's strange expression, she looked about her, trying to find its cause. Funny, they still seemed the same distance from shore. And she must have been rowing for ten or fifteen minutes, if her clamoring body was anything to go by.

With a sinking heart, she glanced around again and discovered the culprit. She'd gotten them caught in a jungle of plant growth.

Afraid to look Cameron in the face, aware now that his pained expression had been one of suppressed laughter, she resumed her rowing, with a singular lack of success. Despite her renewed efforts, Halina could not disentangle the oars, and anywhere she placed them she encountered a verdant flotilla. She silently cursed the owner of the boats, the lake, summer in general—and finally, inescapably, her own inability to get them out of this quandary.

Feeling the perspiration pour down her back, between her breasts, and over her face, she sneaked a look at Cameron. He had remained commendably still during her minor crisis, but she saw the smile, quickly masked as she raised her tired, burning head, still shining out of his laughing eyes.

His calm "Need any help?" was spoken just as she threw injured dignity to the winds and asked, "Think we'll have to swim for it?"

Their gazes met and held, and both started laughing at the same time, the small boat rocking from the force of their combined mirth.

Halina was warmed by his thoughtfulness in offering help before she had been forced to ask for it. The tension was broken and, by the time Cameron had rowed them out of their green prison and onto blessed land, it had totally dissolved.

* * *

After returning the boat, they decided to take a walk before heading back to Lake Villa and home. Halina showed Cameron one of her favorite spots, a secluded wooded area.

When they reached a small clearing, bordered by a myriad of wild flowers whose heady fragrance embodied the sensual haziness of summer, Cameron stopped. He dropped his arm from her waist and stepped back a pace, as if to give Halina a buffer zone.

"Do you think you can tell me now?"

Halina looked at him mutely, trying to comprehend his purpose. He read her again intuitively and told her in a velvet-soft, reassuring tone, "Trust me, Halina. You need to, you know. You can't keep yourself isolated."

His words reached her very soul, tugging at the last shaky defenses. When he said gently, "Halina, that wall is going to smother you. Let it fall. Let it go, sweetheart." She did. Her fortification came tumbling down.

Unconsciously making fists as her arms hung stiffly at her sides, Halina began slowly, haltingly. She told him about her grandparents' deaths, about losing her mother. About the loss of her father's love and support. She explained how he'd chosen to bury his grief in his work, and had never really emerged from his cocoon.

When she began telling Cameron about Jeff, her nails were digging deeply into her palms. Halina noticed it because Cameron came to stand in front of her and, gently prying her hands open, smoothed the palms with slow, easy strokes. Halina stared at the movement of his large secure hands, at the contrast of ivory and bronze.

Her voice gained in strength as she drew warmth from his touch.

With the self-mockery that comes from bitter experience, she told him quietly, "It's amazing, in retrospect, that I was ever attracted to Jeff. I suppose there was some hero worship involved, but I have never been impressed with wealth or status. I guess I craved companionship, and Jeff was there." Staring unseeingly at the golden-green leaves floating in the wind, she said, "He really had me believing he cared. That I was something special to him. Most important, he spent time with me. He shared his thoughts, his plans. And then"—her voice broke, but she smiled and looked directly at Cameron—"when he finally got me into bed, the facade cracked. I didn't satisfy him, he said. I was frigid."

Cameron smoothed her cheek with the back of his hand. "Don't," he said. "He isn't worth it."

"I didn't know that at the time. I'd pinned all my hopes on him, all the starved emotion of an eighteen year old looking for someone to approve of her, to care for her. But I think I could have gotten over it if he hadn't spread the tale around school."

Cameron muttered curses under his breath and Halina turned her cheek into his hand. "Luckily, he was a senior, so I only had to contend with it for one semester. But the offers to 'cure' me that I got from boys who had previously ignored me—well, they were hard to take. I even thought of quitting school."

"But you didn't," Cameron said.

"No, I didn't." Halina took a deep breath and added, "But not solely out of bravery. My father forced me to tell him why all of a sudden I wanted to leave the university I'd been hoping to attend for years, and which I'd been so satisfied with till then."

"What did he say when you told him?"

"The expected. That I had to fight my own battles. That I had walked into the situation with my eyes open. That I couldn't let Jeff drive me out of a college I wanted to stay in. So I stayed, and the following school year everything was more or less forgotten."

"Except by you," Cameron said perceptively.

"Except by me."

"What about Ted?"

"Ted? How did you know about him?"

"Randolph Que mentioned your tennis dates," he explained. "Has Ted hurt you too?"

Halina shook her head. "No," she said softly. "I don't care for him enough that he could hurt me. And he really doesn't care that deeply about me." Moving away from Cameron, Halina said, "For a while there after the episode with Jeff, I didn't date anyone. I'd gone to bed with Jeff once—and that seemed too much. And with all the propositions I'd received, I tended to stay away from them. Then, when I was twenty-three, I became involved with Louis, a visiting lecturer. We met at a reception after a lecture he gave at my college, dated a few times, and I found out that I could no more respond to Louis than I had to Jeff. End of story."

"That's not the end," Cameron told her, turning her to face him. "Were you in love with Louis?"

"No," Halina said. "Louis Davis was a charming urbane man. And a good lover, I'm sure. I found myself attracted to him, hungry for male companionship. I wanted a man and Louis wanted me. But it didn't work out." Looking bravely into his green eyes, she said, "Which is why the few men I've gone out with are Ted's type— the pleasant occasional date that I know poses no danger for me."

"And is that how you intend to lead your life from now on? Safely?" When she didn't answer, he persisted, "You didn't run and transfer out of school when you were a teenager. You stayed and faced all the rumors and fought back. So why are you running now?"

Halina felt pain and wanted to lash out at Cameron. She'd been humiliated and hurt by Jeff, by his friends on the basketball team, by the rumors that had escalated from each individual embellishment. Then, when she'd gathered the courage to allow another man for whom she'd felt affection into her life, all her doubts had re-emerged. And yet here was Cameron, asking her to trust him. Challenging her. What did she know about him?

You knew Jeff and Louis a lot longer, an inner voice prodded. And better. But what difference did it make?

"I guess I'm running because I know that I'm as vulnerable now as I was at eighteen. And I'm afraid of getting hurt again."

Halina barely heard Cameron's muffled expletive, and then he was gathering her into his arms. "Why didn't you tell me about what had happened in your past?" Smiling with self-directed irony, he added, "I can't say the outcome would have been much different, since between my exhaustion and the feelings that had built up in me all evening, I probably could not have lasted any longer. But I could have given you pleasure first."

Coloring at his frankness, Halina said, "It's not something a woman can easily bring into the conversation: 'Oh, by the way, I might be frigid.'"

His arms closed tightly about her, as if to transfer her pain and uncertainty into his body. Halina resisted at first, not wanting pity, but relaxed when he said, "Sweetheart, you're definitely not frigid. You've got me to thank for your regrettable experience. If I hadn't been so weak with desire for you, I would have noticed something was wrong."

Moving away to look down into her eyes, Cameron said softly, "Please, don't be afraid. I'll never hurt you." His face broke into the devastating smile that carved parallel lines in his cheeks, and he promised with wicked humor, "We'll just try it until we get it right. And believe me, I won't mind how long you take—although I have the feeling the third time will be the charm. And just remember, I'd like nothing better than to spend a week in bed with you."

Halina felt his words and tone scald every particle of

her body, and all of a sudden she wanted to be home—
in bed—with him. Cameron must have read her reaction
in her eyes, because he bent his head with a groan,
covering her lips with a kiss that tried to be gentle but
that quickly became one of passionate mutual discovery.
His hands pulled her closer to his body, one hand on
the curve of her bottom, beneath the hem of her brief
shorts, the other in the small of her back, pressing her
lower body into his male hardness, now seeking shelter
against her quivering belly.

They tumbled to the ground, Halina hooking her fingers into his silky black hair, meeting the tender mastery
of his kiss with a passion she hadn't known she possessed. She was lost in the moment, and her heated senses
overflowed with the taste, feel, and smell of him, the
coolness of the grass beneath them, and the intoxicating
scents of summer.

But Cameron's caresses ceased abruptly and he held
her close with punishing strength, stilling her hands when
they would have continued running over his hard aroused
body.

Dropping a feather-light kiss on her mouth, Cameron
helped her up, smiling at her reluctance to leave their
bed of grass. "I feel the same, sweetheart," he told her
in a raspy voice that spoke of his need. "And although
there's nothing I'd like better right now than to make
love to you, I want the experience to be perfect for you,
without fear of interruption."

Stroking her lips, tender and moist from his kisses,
with a gentle finger, he asked, "Will you have dinner
with me tonight in my apartment?"

Halina nodded, unable to speak over the knot of fear
that had suddenly formed in her throat. She wanted Cameron. She could not deny that. But the past still gripped
her with icy tentacles.

Cameron put his arm about her waist and Halina leaned
her head on his chest, keeping her fears silent, still ex-

periencing the inner tremors of unsatisfied passion. He molded her tighter to his hard frame and his reassuring nearness soothed the jangled need within her as they walked slowly back to the car, the gentle breeze cooling their heated damp bodies.

Chapter
9

HALINA PAUSED BEFORE Cameron's door. On the drive back from Lake Villa, she had further explained her feelings of inadequacy and distrust. She smiled as she recalled Cameron's story of his first sexual encounter, which had taken place in a car. He'd been sixteen, on a date with an older girl. What made the episode so amusing was the fact that the only car Cameron had been able to borrow, beg, or steal had been a Volkswagen. And Cameron had reached his magnificent proportions by that time.

She'd known Cameron had exaggerated some details to make things easier for her. And he was certainly frank about how much he wanted her. But as Halina breathed in deeply to quiet her fluttery nerve endings, she was once more assailed with doubts, afraid she would freeze with him again.

Throwing her shoulders back, she knocked. No response. Her hand was upraised to try again when Cameron opened the door, and both his welcoming smile and freshly groomed appearance took her breath away.

"Come in," he invited in a soft, husky purr. "I heard you the first time, but I was in the bedroom, changing the sheets."

Halina gulped and mumbled under her breath, "Said the spider to the fly."

But Cameron heard her. He put a hand on her shoulder and turned her to face him as he closed the door.

"Hey," he said gently, caressing her warm cheeks with

113

one long tender finger. "This is me, remember? I'm not forcing you." Raising his hands, palms forward, he added, "Everything is open and aboveboard. I can't deny I want you like hell, but we'll only make love if *you* want to."

She forced herself to meet and hold his gaze. Cameron was doing everything he could to make her comfortable. He was considering *her* well-being. Jeff had never shown such sensitivity.

"I'm sorry. I guess I'm a bit nervous because I want you so much, and I want to please you . . ."

"But you already have," he said huskily, the blaze that lit up his eyes unnerving her with its intensity. "And you are right now, just by standing there." Taking her trembling hand, he let her know his own was not quite steady. "This is what you do to me. And I hope I'll be able to please you."

He dropped a scorching kiss on her palm and then seemed to put a clamp on his emotions, moving away to a trolley that held liquor, bottles of wine and juice, and a container of ice.

"I'm afraid I don't have anything fancy to offer you. I bought some steaks and made a salad."

"I'm not that hungry right now," she admitted candidly.

He smiled, the lazy quality of it tugging on her nerves with sensual strings. He turned and poured drinks, and when he came toward her she was glancing around the apartment. It was quite bare, the living room containing only an old dilapidated sofa the previous tenants had not even bothered to carry out and a couple of wicker chairs.

"Pretty sad, isn't it?" he said, handing her a tall smoky glass. "I've ordered some more furniture. Since I don't spend too much time in the living room, I just made myself comfortable in the two rooms I use the most."

Halina curved her hands around the cool glass and said with unmasked curiosity, "That reminds me. You were going to tell me something about your background."

"But I did. On the way home, remember?" he said, humor dancing in his eyes.

"That doesn't count," Halina said firmly. "You just shared some of your experiences with women—which was only fair, since I bared my soul to you."

"Oh, there's a lot still to learn about you, Halina Barkley," Cameron said, adding with husky promise in his words, "and I'm willing to take all the time in the world to get to know you better."

"Not fair," Halina insisted. "You already know about my job, my interests..."

"That's only scratching the surface," he told her as he took a sip of his drink. "Mere superficialities. I want to know the real Halina."

"You make me sound like a split personality," Halina said, both nervous and amused. With his perserverance, Cameron should have been a detective.

"In a way you are," he told her, his hand coming up to entwine with hers. "Cool, composed, and capable on the outside; warm, human, and vulnerable inside."

Halina was as shaken at hearing herself described with such accuracy as she was by his disturbing proximity and warm touch. She took a quick sip of her drink and was surprised. She'd been expecting wine.

"Lemonade?" she asked wryly.

His eyes crinkled at the corners and he teased, "Couldn't have you thinking I was plying you with liquor, now, could I?"

As her eyes met his, which were glinting with the humor that seemed ever present, Halina couldn't help but respond to it. Her lips curved into a spontaneous smile and her muscles relaxed.

"Certainly couldn't," she agreed with mock solemnity.

The laughter disappeared from his eyes, replaced by a white-hot brilliance as his glance roved over her with patent hunger. It feasted on her loose chestnut hair, which streamed to her waist in a glossy red-tinted cascade. The straps of the flame-colored sun dress crisscrossed the top curves of her breasts, the low cut revealing the darkened shadow between the ripe firm globes partially concealed by the thick fall of hair.

His lips, still wet from the cool, tangy liquid, descended slowly toward her red mouth, and Halina saw the lambent flames kindled in his eyes before her own closed languorously as she savored the anticipation.

She was not disappointed. His lips stroked hers, rubbing them softly and teasing each corner before he drew her upper lip into his mouth and chewed on it gently, savoring its taste and texture, swelling it into erotic tenderness before repeating the process with her lower lip. Halina hungered for his full possession, her lips tingling with expectation, but he released her mouth to trail cool kisses on her forehead, eyelashes, and nose, stopping for an exquisite instant to touch the tip of his tongue to the spot where a dimple appeared in her right cheek.

He lowered his head to bury it against the full soft pillow of her breasts, his thick hair tickling her throat, his mouth brushing the swell of one breast and then the other, his expert caress peaking them to feverish excitement underneath the double friction of the cotton material and her own silken tresses.

When he licked the shadowed valley, Halina was no longer fully cognizant of her surroundings. One plane of her mind registered that he had somehow gotten rid of their lemonade glasses, and then even that thought fled as he opened the side zipper of her dress and the air-conditioned coolness slipped in the opening.

As Cameron pulled her closer to undo deftly the buttons securing the straps to the back of her dress, his head dipped low again to gently bite a nipple that strained toward him under the exquisitely torturous confinement of the fabric.

Halina could not suppress the moan erupting from her

lips at the intense sensation that sent tongues of fire from her breast to her loins, and to every nerve center in her body. She had rigidly kept her hands at her sides, but now her fists opened and her fingers sought contact with his firm smooth flesh.

The dress slithered down until she stood clad only in lacy flesh-colored bikini panties, and her world turned topsy-turvy as Cameron put one arm under her knees and the other around her waist, swinging her snugly against his body. As he carried her into the bedroom, her hands, which had been stroking the ridged muscles of his chest through his sky-blue silk shirt, slid to his neck.

Her eyes widened as they took in the bed softly bathed in the golden glow of a small lamp. As Cameron stopped, she could not tear her gaze away from its huge roundness. He had obviously replaced the old creaky bed, and this oversized one, covered by a black satin spread, looked imposing even in this, the larger of the two bedrooms.

Her resurging nervousness must have communicated itself to Cameron, because he let her feet slide to the floor and held her loosely in the circle of his arms. Halina looked about her, noticing that the bedroom was now unabashedly masculine, decorated in silver and black.

Her fascinated eyes returned to the bed, which seemed to have grown. Trying to break its mesmerizing effect, Halina told him, "I guess you weren't too busy to get this room ready."

Amused, he said mildly, "I have to sleep sometimes." Pointing toward the closet, he added, deadpan, "I also found time to accomplish one other thing."

Halina's brows rose questioningly and Cameron watched with self-satisfied delight as warmth tinted her face a bright pink when he explained, "In the closet you'll find the chiffon dress you left behind that one morning. Your underwear is in the dresser."

She refused to be embarrassed by the incident, or by the thought of his handling her intimate garments. It seemed ridiculous when she was now joyfully allowing him access to her body. So, rejecting memories of her cowardly flight two weeks ago, she put her arms around his neck and her trust in his keeping.

"You should get a reward for such thoughtfulness," she said provocatively. "As I remember, you had one on account." Placing two quick kisses on firm male lips that softened under hers, she drew back laughingly as Cameron's head bent, following hers as if drawn by a magnet, seeking to renew and lengthen the sweet contact.

"Witch," he murmured against her mouth, his breath and lips a teasing torment.

Hoping to catch him off guard, Halina mentioned casually, "You seem to be so busy—your job must be a demanding one..."

She let her statement trail off inquiringly, and Cameron answered with laughter in his voice, his mouth a mere fraction of an inch from hers. "Just momentarily. I hope to have that side of my affairs terminated soon." Planting a kiss on her rosy cheek, he added with matching casualness, "I think I've found a less stressful way to make a living."

Her gaze flew to his and she saw such tender, knowing amusement in his eyes that her insides began to melt like marshmallows held to fire.

His hand left her back to caress the soft line of her chin and neck. "It's not too late to back out," he told her gently. His mouth returned to hers and rubbed her lips with controlled passion, and then he locked both hands against her lower back, retreating to put a few inches between them. "All you have to do is say the word, and we'll go slowly. We'll take a moonlight ride on Lake Michigan, go to the theater... whatever."

A shiver went through her as the cool air of the room began to chill her back and breasts. Cameron's thoughtfulness reassured her, especially since she knew how much he wanted her. And she wanted him.

The coldness within her was being slowly but surely dissipated by the warmth of his concern and her awareness of his arms around her. All thought processes ceased when he spoke.

"Halina?"

The sound of her name on his lips was gossamer-soft, and her insides began throbbing, an unfamiliar tingling sensation that felt like a million butterflies were sensitizing her, brushing against her with their velvety wings, flutter after delicate flutter.

She leaned her quivering body against his hard aroused length and answered him with her lips, her mouth parting over his and allowing the rough, urgent search of his tongue. His breathing coming in ragged spurts, he took his mouth from hers to bend her over and push the covers back, and then she was floating downward until the slippery coolness of the sheets met her heated skin with a pleasant shock. Halina stretched lazily, no longer wary of the bed but seeking to orient herself to its exotic capaciousness.

Her eyes opened as she felt his body against her side and his mouth nipping at the delicate slope of her shoulder. His hands gently lifted her to slide her lace panties down past the generous curve of her hips and the elegant length of her legs. She knew the desire she saw in his smoldering gaze was replicated in her own. Inching her body closer to his naked frame, she put her arms around his neck and followed the uncontrollable impulse to put her mouth against his scar.

Halina felt him go rigid and raised her head to look into his eyes. "Did I hurt you?" she whispered, not understanding the wariness that darkened his gaze.

Returning the look for an intense moment, he finally relaxed, his lithe body fitting itself once more to her ripe curves. "No," he said, brushing her long hair away from her breasts so he could have an unobstructed view. "No, it doesn't hurt now. But I remember your shocked disgust the first day you saw it, and that, mingled with your pity, was too much."

"Pity! Disgust!" She lifted herself higher, supporting her weight on an elbow as she shook her head at him in disbelief. "So that's why you were so upset. But you're wrong. The only reason I was shocked is because that scar showed you'd had a close brush with death, and meant you must have gone through a lot of pain. I even thought that first day that you might have had a heart operation."

"No," he said thickly as his fingers played with a soft lock of hair that had slid back to cover one alabaster shoulder. "It was a car accident, serious enough that it made me review my life to that point and reconsider the future I'd been given a second chance at." His hand dropped her hair and cupped the back of her head to bring her lips to his. Against her mouth, he whispered, "I might need medical attention for other reasons soon, though, if you don't stop talking. I know anticipation is supposed to heighten lovemaking, but I don't think I can stand any more delays."

"I'm not too crazy about an intermission right now, either," she confessed, and to prove that the scar was not repugnant to her she dropped a quick kiss on his mouth and slid down on the bed, pushing him onto his back while her lips trailed a searing moist line to his scar and all along its wide length.

"Sexy," she murmured, and opened her mouth to let the tip of her tongue touch the reddened rough skin. As she extended the caress with deliberate slowness, Halina felt Cameron's body stiffen, echoing the hardening of the male nipple she had taken delicately between her teeth. She moved across the well-defined chest with sharp love nips, feeling Cameron's heart hammering against the tight skin covered with a springy mat of hair. Her own pulse raced and her heartbeat was a tattoo rever- berating in her ears as she treated the other peak to the same devastating attention, feeling the small knot of flesh press against her teeth.

Supporting herself on her arms, one on each side of the powerful male chest, Halina looked into Cameron's passion-glazed eyes and, without taking her eyes from his, stroked his scar with her silky bosom, brushing lovingly against his taut nipples.

Cameron's body curved convulsively upward and he whispered hoarsely, "Do you know how sensitive my scar is, and what you've just done to me?"

"I think I've just found out," Halina answered with an unrepentant smile, her hand moving with excruciating slowness down his body, making little sensuous forays along the way, her eyes sparkling with the knowledge that her femininity had the power to affect him so strongly.

Grabbing her by the waist, Cameron held her aloft for a moment before reversing their positions and undertaking a sensual attack of his own. Slowly he claimed each inch of her flushed skin as his territory, raising Halina to impossible heights and then retreating again, until she began to writhe beneath him in insupportable sensation, seeking a union with his tormentingly elusive body.

His mouth, which he'd withheld during their love play, started a torturous assault on her lips once more as he lowered himself onto her. Gently separating her thighs with his knee, Cameron slipped both legs between hers, preparing her for his tender exploration.

As his hand sought the vortex of her now consuming desire, touching and gently probing, fanning the brightly burning light of her passion into luminous heat, Halina was conscious of an unfamiliar pulsation within her, a sense of waiting to receive. Cameron remained poised for one timeless instant above her, his eyes locking with hers, meshing their bodies even before he joined them in the ultimate union. As he completed their anxiously awaited linking with consummate care, a soft sound of desire welled in her throat. One hand cradling her head, the other cupping her hip, Cameron stroked deeply at the same instant his tongue invaded the moist cavern of her mouth with lancing, mounting urgency.

Halina responded with fierce untried passion, her body arching to receive him, her moan of satisfaction at the intense, complete filling of her innermost being swallowed by Cameron's mouth. As she sought to increase their cadence, Cameron clasped her firmly and brought her closer to him still, as if they formed one living, breathing entity.

Her breath coming in short sobbing gasps, Halina reached the incandescent summit way before Cameron. He stopped the smooth, measured movement of his hips as her last tremor receded, but kept their bodies joined as she completed her languid, exquisite descent. Before Halina's heartbeat decelerated and her breathing slowed, Cameron began to move once more, probing the deep recesses of her until she was lost again in a swirling river of sensation. She clung to him as the eddy caught her in its unbreakable grip. A wild flood of heat erupted in the nucleus of her body, and Halina's nails dug into his velvety, moist back as it grew to a drowning force and then exploded, diffusing its turbulent liquid fire. The only reality was Cameron, who anchored her with his hands firm on her hips as he was also caught in the scorching torrent. His groans of delight mingled with her cries of ecstasy.

Halina realized with a slowly dawning sense of freedom that indeed there was nothing wrong with her, and that Cameron had just proved how different he was from any other man she'd known. They pleasured each other through the night, Cameron making love to her again and again and receiving her own passion in turn. Sometimes they fulfilled their desire wholly; often he simply caressed her and murmured delicious phrases against the curve of her neck or the twin pillows of her breasts.

Morning's light was creeping in when they were both claimed by a satisfying deep sleep.

Halina woke a few short hours later with a lazy, revitalized kind of energy. She could feel the sun on her closed eyelids, and the reassuring hardness that warmed her side with furnace heat. Cameron's arm was flung over her stomach and its weight felt heavenly on her chilled flesh.

Cameron's head had rested on her breasts during the part of the night they'd actually spent dozing but it was no longer there. She felt it near her shoulder, his thick hair rhythmically caressing her skin as he breathed. She knew he was lying on his stomach.

She was reluctant to open her eyes, wanting to retain the dreamlike quality of the moment. But she could not remain still for long. She needed to stretch. Both of her legs were asleep, the pleasant anchoring of Cameron's thigh now an unwitting torture.

Carefully edging away from Cameron, trying to retrieve her legs without awakening him, Halina breathed a silent and premature sigh of relief. It immediately turned into a loud yelp as she stretched her arms above her head and extended her legs to relieve their cramping—and promptly found herself on the floor, her torso, already hanging precariously on the bed's rounded edge, overbalanced by arms and legs that flailed uselessly in the empty air.

Her thud on the uncarpeted floor and her accompanying shriek brought Cameron's tousled head over the side of the bed. As she lay on the floor, nursing a bit more than injured dignity, he asked with sleepy interest, "Is that a daily ritual of yours—bouncing from the bed with such energy? Or are you one of those morning people who can't stand to see others cozy under the covers long after sunup?"

Halina hurled one of the slippers she spied under the

bed in his direction. Cameron ducked quickly and she leaped up, running for the bathroom.

"Hey, come back here!" His disgruntled call made her lock the bathroom against him and she laughed softly, taunting him from the safety of the other side, "You'd better keep it down, or you'll get a complaint from the landlady."

"Seems I've heard this before," he muttered, but Halina detected amusement mingled with frustration in his voice and her lips curved into a tender smile.

She delivered a parting shot before turning on the shower and drowning out his response. "Well, it just shows you don't learn from past mistakes."

Halina took a long, luxurious shower and emerged squeaky clean and wrinkled from the prolonged exposure to the steaming water. As she was rubbing her hair dry with Cameron's forest-green towel, she realized with surprise that she could hear no noise from the bedroom. Intrigued, she wrapped the thick velvety bath towel around herself and knotted it securely to free both hands for any attack that might be forthcoming as she opened the door.

But the room was empty. She called his name, and when Cameron didn't answer, she checked the dresser. Her key was gone.

Dressing quickly, Halina hurried out of Cameron's room, shaking her head at her failure to foresee what he'd do. Rather than wait until she finished her lengthy shower, he'd gone over to her apartment to make use of her bathroom. Or, she thought guiltily, he might be waiting in her bedroom.

An eager smile on her lips, she opened the unlocked door to her apartment and saw her key on the small table near the entrance. She ran into the bedroom, tingling with anticipation, and saw that it was empty—except for the note on the powder-blue bedcover.

The smile faded and then returned with a rueful quality as she realized that Cameron had given her some of her own medicine. His note showed how well he knew her teasing temperament:

> Halina, I know you'll be in that bathroom for as long as you can stand it. So I came over to use yours. I need to go into the office for a while, but I'd like to see you later today. How about a game of tennis? If you can make it, please meet me at the Midtown at four.
>
> P.S. Next time you won't be in that shower alone.
>
> CKC

It was that last line that made Halina consider whether she should meet him at all. Briefly she contemplated not showing up, to pay him back for his own disappearing act. But Cameron had tolerated a couple of her stunts with commendable patience and restraint. She had always admired a sense of humor in a man—especially when it involved the capacity to laugh at oneself. And Cameron had proven he could laugh at himself. It didn't threaten his masculinity. Besides, Halina reflected as she changed into shorts and a T-shirt and got out her briefcase, if she didn't go, she would certainly be cutting off her nose to spite her face. So, swallowing her empty pride, she decided to meet him.

Chapter

10

CAMERON WAS ALREADY on the court when Halina got to the tennis club. She watched him for a moment, observing his unorthodox serve: His feet left the floor completely as he shot forward into the court, his shoulder rolling into one smooth, powerful motion.

After looking on silently for only a couple of minutes, Halina winced. If his serve were timed, Cameron would probably be clocked at well over a hundred miles an hour. Halina considered herself a powerful server, but because she was a woman and of average height, she was handicapped against a strong male opponent. Cameron would blow her off the court.

She approached him slowly, her tennis shoes making no noise on the hard slick surface. Her eager eyes took in the shapely male legs and tight buttocks in the brief whites molding them, and the way the black-and-white top hugged his wide, rippling back and shoulders. She felt a flash of heat as she recalled thinking that Cameron would be breathtaking in a tennis outfit. He seemed to sense her presence in the middle of his service motion, and he turned to face her after completing it with athletic grace.

Halina noticed how his eyes gleamed as they took in her flaring lilac skirt and lilac-and-pink top, and her velvety calves and thighs as she came to a stop scant inches from him. She thought his eyes remained a fraction of a second longer on the slight swell of breast visible over her tank top, and was glad that he seemed as fascinated by her form as she was by his.

But a closer look at his face revealed that he was already perspiring. Remembering the awful worry of that night she'd nursed him, Halina asked anxiously, "Are you all right? How long have you been warming up?"

"I'm fine, Mother," he mocked her, his voice that of a dutiful child answering a fussing parent. "About fifteen minutes."

"Do you think you should be playing? You never did explain about your accident . . ."

"Wouldn't want to bore you with the details," he said, sidestepping her search for an explanation with infuriating ease. "But yes, I definitely should be starting to play again. I've been far too lazy, and I find I'm quite out of shape."

Halina bit back her comment that he certainly did not look out of shape to her. Ignoring his charming smile, she answered instead with definite irritation, "You'd better know what you're doing, because I've never wanted to be a private nurse. And since I have to work tomorrow, I don't intend to stay up all night taking care of you."

Walking off in a huff that disguised her concern, Halina threw her bag to one side and unzipped the cover of her wood racket. She noticed Cameron had an oversized graphite, and thought sourly that he must use it just to impress his partners.

Wanting to dissipate some of her anger at his pigheadedness, she practiced a few serves, but her form and timing were off. The knowledge that *he* was watching made her nervous, and she either netted her serves or hit them long or wide.

She finally turned to him and hissed, "Would you stop staring at me?"

"Why? You were looking me over for quite a long time," he said innocently.

"Why didn't you acknowledge my presence?"

"Why didn't you say hello?"

His sensible question neatly cut off her indignant attack. And since she didn't particularly want to admit to this already overconfident, overbearing male that she had enjoyed the play of masculine muscle and sinew in a sport that so elegantly combined agile power and grace, she let it pass. After a few more anemic serves, Halina told Cameron she was ready.

Halina won the flip of the coin and elected to serve, assuring Cameron that she didn't need more of a warm-up. He took the first game at love, playing mostly from the baseline, passing her with shots that whizzed by like bullets.

Throwing him a grim forced smile, Halina told herself that she just needed to find her groove. After all, she had consistently won local tournaments in both singles and doubles, and had beaten Ted Lander more times than he would like to remember. And although Ted was not in Cameron's league, he was certainly no lightweight.

But her pep talk proved useless. Cameron won the second game with a blistering first serve on which he came in each time, and a couple of aces. By the time Cameron broke her serve for the second time and had the advantage, leading 3–love, Halina began finding resources she didn't know existed. She took the fourth game to deuce, then got the advantage with an ace, and finally won her first game of the first set.

Cameron saluted her with his racket after she hit a particularly fine lob and came in when Cameron chased it down and barely got his racket on it for a defensive return. She won the game with a well-placed half volley.

Her adrenaline pumping, Halina dipped into her bag of tricks and began playing brilliantly, trying dink shots and top spins but avoiding the lobs, because she wasn't able to surprise Cameron again and it was difficult to get past his height and athletic reach.

Cameron ended up taking the first set 7–5, but Halina

won the next two, 6–4 and 6–3. She could tell he was tiring, but Cameron insisted on playing a few more sets.

Halina became sharper as they played, and she was able to move Cameron around the court, as he'd previously done with her. She was a serve-and-volley player, but found she could not fit Cameron onto a comfortable peg; although he was an excellent ground stroker, when he did rush the net after his powerful first serves, he was lethal. He didn't have a glaring weakness, and Halina marveled at his blasting single-handed backhand, his best tool. She used a two-handed one herself, but although her accuracy was outstanding, she wished uncharacteristically for a man's strength—especially his.

In his last games Cameron played mostly from the baseline, and Halina knew he was going solely on willpower. But she also knew it was useless to tell him anything—he was as stubborn as she was.

Taking her time while serving during their last set, Halina dried her dripping face with her wristband and breathed deeply, amazed at her competitiveness with this man. She netted her first serve as she realized that Cameron aroused her competitive spirit because of the professional way he played. He was not patronizing; he appreciated a good shot, even from his opponent. Also, he didn't let her win, as some of the men she'd dated had tried to do at first, until they found out she played better than they did. Then they'd backtrack and try to retrieve their egos, and would get nasty or churlish about their losses.

After double-faulting twice, Halina went to her bag for her towel and dried her face, hands, and arms. The brief respite renewed her determination. As she resumed her serving position, Halina remembered her mother's advice, reinforced by her grandmother—that she should always do her best.

But her best wasn't good enough. Cameron returned

one of her finest serves, which touched the line, and passed her with a cross-court forehand that caught her too near the net. Although she lunged for it, she was barely able to get the top of her racket on it, and she ended up falling facedown.

Cameron immediately started moving forward, calling "Are you all right?" in a concerned tone.

Halina waved him back, telling him she was fine, and finished the game, the minor scraping not causing her much discomfort. She was used to it; she always chased every ball, and giving a hundred percent meant a few tumbles here and there.

Her concentration was off during their last few games. Halina was elated that Cameron's talk of fair play was not just lip service; he actually did treat her as an equal. She'd had to duck a few times when he'd aimed balls straight at her body, as had he when hers had come dangerously close to him. He also dropped balls at her feet whenever the opportunity arose.

As they approached the net to shake hands, Halina having lost the final set but carrying a 2 – 1 lead, Cameron congratulated her, warmly complimenting her skill.

"I would appreciate one thing, though," he told her as they got their tennis gear together.

Halina looked up at him questioningly and he smiled with wicked mischief. "Please watch the direction of the ball. I'd like to have children someday. And, of course, I also have very immediate plans for that area you almost flattened."

"I think your ego should be flattened," she retorted, swinging her bag onto her shoulder and drying some remaining moisture from her face. "You know body shots are perfectly legal — you used them yourself. And I'd like to remind you that you seem to take a lot for granted."

"Am I taking a lot for granted?"

When she walked down the steps and strode across

the parking lot without answering, he grabbed her arm and, swinging her around, embraced her and kissed her with insistent passion.

Halina at first resisted the stiff pressure on her neck that kept her head in place for his kiss. But when he softened his grip and his mouth on hers began to communicate coaxing tenderness rather than hard possession, her own lips acquiesced and opened under his. His right hand rubbed the junction of neck and shoulder, finding the sensitive spot that made her shiver from the sensual tickle, and his left hand lowered to her hip, pressing her body into his.

When she found her arms going around the narrow masculine waist and her fingers instinctively sliding down to grip the hard, fleshy lower torso, Halina suddenly realized where they were. Bringing a hand between their bodies and pushing at his chest, Halina was finally able to make Cameron cognizant of his surroundings also.

"Do you still think I'm taking too much for granted?" he breathed against her cheek.

Halina wedged her elbows between them and looked up at him with fire in her eyes. She had never liked male arrogance, and was not about to tolerate it from Cameron. But when she met his amused glance, she knew he'd been trying to get a rise out of her for her remark. Biting back the ready words on her tongue, she told him suggestively, "I think you should try finding out in a less public place."

"Then let's get going," Cameron said with pleasing alacrity, putting his arm around her waist and fairly lifting her off the ground as they walked to her car. When he bent to lick her salty neck, Halina squealed, a violent shiver coursing through her body.

"Stop it," she said as he showed every intention of repeating the erotic little action. "Give me a chance to shower first."

"I like honest sweat," Cameron told her as he saw her

seated in her car. He added as he fitted his length next to hers, "You not only smell terrific, you taste delicious."

She tried to look severe and forbidding, but it was hard; lately, all she felt like doing was smiling. Although Cameron was something of an enigma and definitely a challenge, Halina felt revitalized and happily alive with him. She was a little dazed by the speed with which Cameron had demolished her preconceived notion of him, and she could recall neither her initial indifference nor subsequent hostility with ease.

"You're impossible," she chided him.

His high-voltage grin started her heart hammering as she turned on the ignition and backed the car up. To quiet its hectic beating, she asked a question that had been stored in the back of her mind for a while. "How come you don't have a car? Was the accident so bad you don't want to drive, or do you just dislike Chicago traffic?"

"Ever curious, aren't you?" he said with a teasing grin.

"Don't I have the right to be? Or am *I* taking too much for granted?" she shot back.

His smile dimmed and a thoughtful look came into his eyes. "No. You do have a right to know, and I'll tell you about the accident over dinner."

"What about the rest?" she asked, pressing her advantage. "Why you really came to Chicago, why you decided to rent in my building, what your job is . . ."

"Whoa, there, lady," he said in a good Texan drawl. "I have to keep you coming back for more. Tonight you'll get another installment in the life and times of Cameron Kirk Connors."

"Cameron Kirk Connors," she repeated slowly, expertly pulling into the fast lane. "I wondered what the *K* stood for. I like the sound of it."

"And I like the way it sounds on your lips," he said huskily, his eyes devouring the outline of her mouth, which she licked in a self-conscious movement. She had very rarely driven on dates, and when she had, she'd been able to do so with her usual skill. But having Cameron next to her made it impossible to act naturally, and Halina had to concentrate doubly hard to keep driving smoothly.

When his hand closed on her thigh she jumped, but was able to keep her foot on the brake. After circling a taxi driver who tried to pass her and cut her off, she threw Cameron an accusing look. "Will you keep your hands off while I'm driving? You're making it awfully hard to concentrate."

"Good," he pronounced smugly. "This will give you a taste of what it does to a man to have to concentrate when the woman snuggling up to him is driving him mad." His hand moved back and forth on her leg, establishing a path of fire between knee and upper thigh. "I must say, I rather like being chauffeured around."

Halina gritted her teeth and endured the sweet torture, telling herself that at least his hand was not straying underneath her brief skirt. Then she would have had to pull to the side of the road.

The rest of the trip was conducted in silence, which was almost unbearable for her, though obviously very enjoyable for Cameron.

"How about some pizza?" Cameron asked as he opened the door to his apartment and stepped aside to let Halina precede him. "We'll have it delivered. Why should we have to bother with such mundane details as cooking?"

"What details *were* you interested in?" she asked, leaning on the door after he closed it.

Cameron put his right hand by her face on the polished wood and ran his left lightly down the front of her body, from shoulder to thigh. "I'm interested in all these irresistible places I was not allowed to touch while you were driving."

"Well, you just did," Halina told him, gray eyes shining with mischief as she straightened from the door. "I'll just go take a shower while you order a peperoni pizza."

But she found her path cut off as Cameron put up his other hand, trapping her neatly between both arms.

"There's two things wrong with your suggestion," he said lazily.

"Really?" Halina said. "I thought it made a lot of sense."

Cameron shook his head, the movement bringing a mass of straight black hair down over a thick eyebrow. Halina raised her hand to push it back, caught his look, and pushed a tendril of her own hair nonchalantly behind her ear, smiling smugly.

"First," he said, leaning his body into hers and watching her smug look crack little by little, "I like mushrooms on my pizza..."

"That's easily remedied," she told him, pushing at his shoulders. "By all means, let's get peperoni *and* mushrooms."

"Second," he said as he let his lower body push gently against her belly and thighs, *"you* won't be taking a shower. *We* will."

"I thought you were going to tell me about your car accident," she reminded him dryly.

"All in good time," he told her, beginning to nuzzle her neck.

She tried to evade his seeking mouth, but it unerringly found a sensitive target. Her breathing began to quicken. Halina said, "I want information."

"And I want you."

"All you think of is bed."

Withdrawing his mouth from her shoulder, where he'd left a series of love nips, Cameron asked her throatily, "And what's running through your mind now?"

As his hand smoothed the side of her thigh, which instinctively strained against the hair-roughened length of his, Halina said slowly, "Well...I was thinking in

terms of a crisp thin crust, topped by a deluge of toma-
to sauce, smothered by a thick layer of mozzarella,
and—"

Her words were abruptly cut off as Cameron picked
her up and started toward the bathroom with her, his
mouth covering hers in a quick, tender punishment for
her teasing.

Kicking the door fully open, he walked to the large
bathtub and stood her in it, keeping one arm around her
waist as he turned on the cold water.

"Why, you monster," Halina spluttered. "My
clothes..."

"I'll take them to the dry cleaner in the morning," he
promised as he stepped into the bathtub with her, tennis
shoes and all.

"At this rate you'll run up quite a bill," Halina told
him, her teeth beginning to chatter. She tried to stop the
hands that went to the fastening of her skirt, but with no
success.

He quickly disposed of her tennis outfit and bent to
remove the shoes. His mouth found her navel above the
line of her bikini briefs and he licked it sensuously, the
warmth of his tongue combining with the biting coldness
of the water in an almost unbearable sensation.

"Cameron, it's freezing. Do you intend for us to catch
pneumonia?" she complained, her voice unsteady as he
turned his attention from her shoes to her briefs.

"It won't be freezing for long," he answered, casually
discarding the tiny bit of lace over the edge of the tub
and turning his full attention to her trembling length. "I'll
warm you first, then I'll go order the pizza."

Thirty minutes later, Halina found herself again in
Cameron's arms—this time en route to his round bed.
He deposited her, wet and shivering from his ministra-
tions, on the welcome dryness of the white-on-black

sheets. The only towel he allowed was the large one wrapped around her abundant hair.

But he removed even that one, put one knee on the bed, and vigorously rubbed the moisture from the long strands. Apparently satisfied with his results, he buried his fingers in the red-brown silkiness and then brought the ends of her hair to his face, rubbing them against his cheek.

"You smell terrific," he told her huskily, inhaling deeply.

Halina pushed herself up and told him dryly, "You should know. You washed and rewashed every inch of me."

"As I recall, I didn't hear any complaints," he said, wrapping her hair around his hands and drawing her gently close to him.

"I was numb with shock. Cold does funny things to me," she retorted swiftly, her face now only an inch from his. "And I've never seen anyone put through an order for pizza in such record time," she added as she ran her own fingers through Cameron's hair, the velvety dampness tickling.

"Couldn't take a chance you'd leave the bathtub," he told her, brushing his lips lightly against hers. "As it was, you'd turned the hot water on by the time I got back."

"And you turned it back to cold right away," she reminded him as she kissed his earlobe. "That was a cruel thing to do."

"Considering the results, I'd say the side effects were minimal."

He let go of her hair and was pushing her back onto the bed when the phone rang. Ignoring it, he completed the motion and followed her down.

When the ringing stopped, then began again insistently, Cameron groaned. "Don't you think you'd better answer?" Halina asked, amused.

He swore under his breath, and Halina was not too thrilled with the intrusion herself.

Cameron jumped off the bed and strode to the phone in the living room, his body rigid with anger. His "Connors here" was not the height of civility, but his tone softened somewhat as he said, "Yes, Carol . . . I've been out all day."

Impatience was obvious in his voice when he interrupted the woman after a lengthy pause. "Carol, I'm busy at the moment. Next week is fine, but I'll call you tomorrow about the details. Good night."

Halina watched him with a puzzled expression as he came back into the room.

"You get business calls this late?" she asked curiously.

Walking to the side of the bed, Cameron grabbed her waist and pulled her to him in one fluid movement. "I'm going to be working out of my home. Carol is one of my clients—a dear one, in fact, but she has one major flaw: She talks too much."

"I noticed you didn't give her much of a chance for that," she told him laughingly as he bore her back to the bed again.

"You're more important to me than any business," he said in a voice raspy with need. "But we won't be bothered again. I left the phone off the hook."

His lips had begun to seek hers when the doorbell rang. His mouth opened, ready to let loose a tirade, Halina was sure. But he clamped it shut and moved away from her with resignation. "The pizza."

Halina was not able to restrain the laughter that bubbled forth. "You—you—" she gasped, and then tried again. "You don't seem to have much luck tonight."

He gave her a fierce kiss before leaving the bed once more. Picking up the discarded bath towel from the floor, he carelessly threw it around his hips.

"Let's hope the delivery boy is not a girl," she called after him in a voice still choked with laughter.

"Whoever it is," he flung at her over his shoulder, "won't take too long when they see they've interrupted important business."

Halina jumped off the bed and put on one of his shirts, which reached the rounded tops of her thighs. She was about to head for the kitchen when Cameron came back in.

"Where do you think you're going?" he asked, pulling off the green towel in a disgusted movement.

"The pizza—" she began, her own movements aborted.

Cameron walked over to her and began to open the few buttons she'd managed to close. "The pizza can wait."

"Don't I have any say as to when I get fed around here?" Halina asked heatedly.

"You can eat anytime," he told her in a voice that made her shiver. "But our time together has been too scarce—and we don't need any interruption now."

As he pulled the shirt from her shoulders, Halina found that the needs of her stomach took a backseat to others he was creating. She put her hands about his waist in tacit agreement with his priorities.

An hour later Halina came out of the bathroom again looking rosily clean and fresh, and found Cameron on the living room couch, a thick quilt over its torn cover. "You and your showers," he mock-grumbled. Eyeing his white robe on her ripe curves, he asked, "And don't you think you're overdressed for the occasion?"

Halina looked at the towel hanging precariously low on his narrow hips and told him dryly, "One of us should be decently covered. I'd like to eat the pizza this time."

As he brought her down on his lap when she reached the couch, she added firmly, "And I'd like to hear all about the accident—and your job. You've kept me in suspense long enough."

"Spoilsport," he chided, but kept his hands on her waist.

Leaning against the back of the couch gingerly to avoid being scratched by rough patches in the upholstery, he settled her snugly against his bare chest and began recounting his accident.

It had taken place late at night on a narrow Texas road near Karnes City as he was returning home after some business in Kingsville.

"I was stubborn, deciding to drive back that night against the advice of associates," he said with biting self-mockery. "I was very single-minded, worrying only about the expansion of our business. When my father suggested I take the company plane, I told him I didn't need it, that I felt like driving and working some problems out in my mind." Curving his hand around the long column of her neck, he murmured, "I do some of my best work at night."

Halina pulled his hand away from her receptive flesh, determined to keep both of them cool until he finished his story to her satisfaction. Holding his large hand captive in her own smaller one, she told him silkily, "You're not bad in the mornings, either." When his hand began to slide from her grasp, she grabbed it with both of hers and told him severely, "The story, please. No story, no playing."

Cameron sighed and continued, "Being the all-knowing fool that I was, I ended up falling asleep at the wheel. I woke up just in time to see I'd veered into the other side of the road, in front of an oncoming car. I managed to avoid hitting the car, but crashed full speed into a tree."

Halina's hands tightened convulsively around his as her horrified mind pictured the scene. Cameron's other hand left her waist to caress her arm, patting it soothingly. "I deserved what I got—and more, even. I was lucky to get out alive."

"Were the people in the other car okay?" Halina asked in a worry-roughened voice.

Cameron nodded. "Although I floated in and out of consciousness, I'll never forget those images. The man sent his wife and two children to get help, and he stayed behind to try to stop the flow of blood from the rip in my chest while avoiding embedding the piece of metal any further into the flesh.

"When the ambulance came, the man was still there, standing with his wife and two children, covered with the blood of the driver who had almost taken his and his family's lives. And I never even found out his name, to thank him."

"I'm sure the man was grateful himself that you managed to prevent causing him and his family harm. You only injured yourself," Halina told him quietly, trying to erase the raw pain she saw contorting his face.

"Through sheer luck," Cameron said grimly. "I had no business on that road that night. I'd been pushing myself too hard, worrying about corporate policy a hell of a lot more than I was concerned about my personal life. I worked hard and I played hard. And I paid the price. The miracle is that I got a second chance."

"Were you very ill?"

"The doctor told me later I'd had one chance in three of pulling out of it. While I was convalescing at a friend's ranch near San Antonio, looking at all the beauty and peaceful life around me, I realized what I'd almost gambled away." Taking her hands, as if to seek solace himself now, he told her in a low voice that didn't completely hide his anguish, "What really kept me from sleeping, though, was not the hellish pain. It was nightmares about those two children. They couldn't have been more than seven and they were bathed in blood. I woke time and time again, covered in cold sweat, screaming a warning to that family—and always being too late."

The tears she saw brightening Cameron's pained eyes brought some to her own. She squeezed his hands, trying to offer comfort. To divert his attention from the relived nightmares, she asked, "How long were you at your friend's ranch?"

"Five weeks. The doctor told me I should have stayed longer, but I wanted to take care of a few things before coming to Chicago. That's why I was so weak when I first got here—although the stimulation you've provided seems to have done me a world of good."

Ignoring his husky teasing, she said, "What kind of business were you in?"

"And I thought I was single-minded," Cameron said, humor and impatience threading his voice.

But Halina saw that some of the pain that had shadowed his eyes had receded. She leaned forward to kiss him softly, her lips tasting the salty wetness of his lashes.

Although a flame of desire leaped to his gaze at her action, Cameron did not pull her against him, as she knew he wanted to do. She was also pleased that he had not been ashamed of showing his hurt. She felt tenderness wash over her at the thought that he had suffered more from guilt because he'd almost caused death than from his own excruciating physical pain.

Cameron continued slowly, "My father was an engineer, a damn good one. He invented a product, and when no one would market it, he decided to do it himself. So he worked hard to secure some capital and then borrowed some more, going into debt to the hilt. By the time he was ready to found his company I'd finished my M.B.A., and his electronic invention caught on like wildfire."

"Did you enjoy your work?" she asked. "Or were you

just trying to help your father out?"

"Oh, I wanted to help my father fulfill his dream, but I wouldn't have come back after I got my Ph.D. in economics if I hadn't liked it. I thrived on the challenge, the complexities of big business, the thrill of gambling on acquisitions."

Shifting slightly on the couch, he scissored her legs so that they lay one on each side of his body, and he continued, "But all of a sudden the new branch in Houston I'd supervised since its inception, the company's headquarters in Dallas, and my own baby in Austin just didn't seem so important. I decided to review my life, to put things in persepctive."

"So you decided to come back to Chicago," she said, feeling warmth travel from his body to her inner thighs.

"When the doctor told me I'd been on the verge of collapse from exhaustion, and that I'd better take a few months off from the competitive world of business, I thought coming back to my old neighborhood would do the trick." His hand lowering to caress her knee, he added huskily, "Meeting you clinched it."

"Shouldn't the pizza be hot by now?" she asked him as he showed no indication of stopping his sensuous journey.

As his hand went to her robe, he answered unconcernedly, "Probably."

Softly gliding her hands over the smooth muscles of his arms, Halina waited until they reached his shoulders, and then, gaining a hold, she pushed away from him and quickly slid off his thighs.

"Then let's eat."

Cameron looked at her lazily, his large frame indolently sprawled on the couch, whose springs sagged under his weight, and he said with weary patience, "All right. You win. We'll eat."

Not trusting his deceptively slow movements, Halina

cautiously stepped away from his reach. But Cameron made no move to grab her. He merely strode off in the direction of the kitchen.

Halina sat in the middle of the couch again, reviewing all she'd recently heard. The aromatic spiciness of the pizza announced Cameron's arrival, and she watched the play of muscles as he set the tray with food and drinks on the walnut coffee table.

Halina leaned forward to serve Cameron and herself a slice of the luscious-looking pizza, but Cameron sat down next to her and, in a quick motion, restored her to his lap.

Opening the tightened white sash of the robe a bit, he pulled the lapels open so that her luxuriant femininity was partially revealed. Then, putting his hands inside and pushing the material aside, he cupped her breasts and dropped a kiss on each coral bud, bringing them instantly to diamond-hardness.

"Cameron," Halina reproved in a strangled voice. She removed his hands and said, "You haven't finished telling me about your job—about what you do now."

"I only promised to tell you about the accident. The rest can wait."

"There's still the pizza," she said, beginning to close the front of her robe. But at his look she left it looser, to try and prevent his rummaging inside again.

"That's better," he said approvingly, his eyes gleaming.

"I've learned to compromise," she said archly. When she attempted to move forward again to reach the pizza, Cameron once more rearranged her legs around him. Sliding the coffee table closer, he picked up a slice, holding it temptingly in front of her mouth.

"I'm starving," she protested, resenting his persistence at the same time as her body welcomed her erotic position.

"So am I," Cameron said in a gritty, dangerous purr. "So I'll feed your hunger first, and then you can feed mine." As he languidly stroked her thigh, he asked her, "How's that for compromise?"

"I'm too weak to argue," she finally whispered, her teeth biting into the fragrant, tasty crust as her hand went to his chest to begin a counterattack of her own.

Chapter
11

HALINA WAS ABLE to finish her counseling session sooner than she'd expected, since only two of her three students had been able to keep their appointments. She raced home, something she hadn't done in a long time.

After her father had died, there had not been anyone waiting for her; and although Halina liked the independence and freedom of her life, there were times when her apartment felt a bit too empty. But she'd always been an active person, so between her work at school, the building, and her sports, she'd been able to fill those voids—or at least keep busy enough to ignore them.

Excitement kept her at a fever pitch while she bathed and dressed in record time, the cream skirt and light matching sweater a concession to the cooler weather.

She decided to surprise Cameron. Rather than call and let him know she was home ahead of time, she took her key chain and, after locking her door, hurried on trembling legs to his apartment.

Taking a deep breath to calm her mounting agitation, she opened the door noiselessly with a slightly unsteady hand, smiling at the door's cooperation. Stepping inside and closing the door carefully, she walked farther into the room. And stopped dead at the sight of a brunette coming out of the bathroom, which divided the two bedrooms. The woman didn't notice her, answering Cameron's call from the room to her left. Halina registered with detachment that the brunette's melodious voice was as attractive as the rest of her.

Some part of her mind took over then, automatically directing her steps to the door. She did not wish to be discovered.

With leaden hands and feet, Halina went through the motions of opening and closing his door and unlocking her own. Once in the haven of her apartment, Halina sat down in her rocking chair and carefully leaned her head back, as if the most minute action would disturb her fragile composure.

She never knew afterward just how long she'd rocked in the old comforting chair, its soothing movement bringing to mind the times her mother had rocked her in it, holding her in the warm safety of her lap as she either talked or willed her pains and troubles away.

Only now she didn't have her mother, or her grandmother—or even her father to lend an absent ear. Hal Barkley had been there for her when she'd really needed him that one time.

What had happened to her as a teenager was over and done with. And Cameron had helped her get over the ghosts and fears in her past. For that, she would always be grateful.

What she could not understand was Cameron's deception. What possible business could he have with that woman that needed to be conducted in his apartment? The words he'd used—". . . less stressful way to make a living"—to describe his new job floated into her mind. But Halina quickly discarded the images his description evoked. She would not believe that of Cameron.

And yet there was still the presence of the brunette to be explained. Cameron had acted as if he couldn't wait to see her again. But he had someone else in his apartment. He'd not mentioned love, although Halina had thought she was nearly in love with him. She now told herself it was merely infatuation, the type female patients developed for their doctors. Because, in a sense, she realized, Cameron had acted as a practitioner, forcing her to confront her confusion and uncertainty, helping her toward self-discovery with exquisite tenderness and understanding.

Now she felt complete, fulfilled, though afraid again, for a very different reason. She could just not reconcile the Cameron that had taught her the magic and mutuality of lovemaking, the man who'd had tears in his eyes when recounting his accident, with a man capable of falseness.

But it seemed that this man she'd thought straight-forward and honest, a man who had taken her to the heights of sensual feeling, was now unwittingly bringing her down to the loneliest depths.

Without knowing what time it was, Halina unfolded her cramped form from the chair and took the phone off the hook. Taking her skirt and sweater off, she left her slip and panties on and tumbled into bed, pushing all jumbled thoughts of her childhood, Jeff, her father, and Cameron out of her tired mind. She curled up into a tight ball and grabbed her pillow with fingers that went numb with her effort to keep her tears at bay.

A few hours later Halina was startled awake by a nightmare. The pale fingers of dawn were threading their way into the room, dappling the carpeting and bedspread. She rubbed her eyes tiredly as the events of the previous night attacked her consciousness. Blindly searching for her robe, she got up slowly.

As she walked toward the kitchen to make herself a strong cup of coffee, she froze. Cameron was sleeping on her couch, his sport jacket thrown over the back of it along with a striped tie, his brown shirt opened at the neck. Looking at his strong chiseled profile, she found it impossible to believe he could be capable of hypocrisy. But Halina had witnessed it, and although she had no right to call his actions a betrayal—he'd made no commitment and neither had she—it still felt that way to her.

Steeling her heart and her senses against his magnetic pull, Halina approached him silently. As she shook him awake, she couldn't help but wonder at his peaceful sleep. It looked as if nothing was bothering his conscience.

Cameron's sleepy eyes opened and pinned her with a penetrating stare. The anger changed swiftly to concern as he saw the pale face and the dark circles beneath her eyes.

"Are you all right?" he asked as he jumped from the couch in a fluid movement.

Halina automatically took a step backward. She feared his disturbing proximity.

"Yes, I am," she lied. Her head seemed to be splintering in a thousand pieces. "About yesterday..."

"You look like hell to me," he interrupted aggressively. "But by all means, tell me about yesterday," he added in a softer tone as her trembling hand went unconsciously to her forehead.

"I'm sorry I didn't call you. I meant to, but I guess I fell asleep."

The small silence that ensued was electric. Halina felt her mouth dry up, and she swallowed convulsively.

"I see," he said tonelessly. "You didn't think to call me, knowing I would be half out of my mind with worry over you, waiting for you to come over, first thinking your counseling had taken longer than expected and then trying to call you at home because the switchboard was not working at the college."

"Yes, well..." Halina tried again weakly, surprised at the intensity of emotion Cameron was displaying. Anyone would think she was the one who should feel guilty. She even began to, until she recalled again the woman in his apartment. She had no interest in the women in Cameron's past. But the present was very much her business. She could never close her eyes to it.

She was tempted to ignore her pride and confront him

with what she'd seen, but he continued relentlessly, "And you didn't stop to think what finding the phone off the hook might mean to me?" His hands twitched at his sides, as if he wanted to shake her. "And then I decided to use your extra key and found you facedown on your bed. Didn't you think what my reaction would be then?"

Halina shook her head helplessly, the pain in her temples and neck and his torrent of recriminations equally punishing. "My heart almost stopped, lady. When I realized you were just sleeping, and had thought of taking the phone off the hook but not of giving me a call, I could have . . ."

He stopped and took a deep breath, then began pacing furiously, as if to work off his anger. Halina looked at him with a curious detachment, thinking that his anger probably involved his ego. He couldn't be experiencing the pain that had knifed her yesterday in his apartment.

"Don't ever do that to me again, Halina, I warn you," he told her with soft fury. "I don't know what sort of game you were playing yesterday . . ."

"You warn *me!"* she shouted, blood flowing in her veins with welcoming fierceness. "How dare you! As for playing games, you—"

Biting her lips savagely, Halina turned her back on him, suppressing the words that threatened to burst out. Ignoring the pounding in her skull, she forced herself into calmness, determined to get him out of her apartment before she broke down.

His voice right behind her startled her. "Yes, what about me?" His tone had an expectant quality, but Halina was past the point where she had any desire or ability to read nuances.

"Never mind," she said flatly. "I think we should stop seeing each other."

"Stop seeing each other," he enunciated slowly, as if the words were somehow incomprehensible to him. "Why on earth. . . . You couldn't wait to make love with me after our tennis game," he told her brutally. "You couldn't have changed your mind so radically."

"Well, you know what they say about sports," she retorted defensively. "They put fire in the blood."

"And that's not your type of action either," he said harshly. "Don't demean what we have together."

Halina lowered her eyes under the rebuke in his. "Cameron, please go," she said softly, at the end of her tether. "I need time to think things over. And regardless of what you may say, I think we should stop seeing each other." To appease him, she added, "At least for a while."

"So I don't have a say in the matter." His tone was so bitter that her eyes flew to his, but his face was an impassive mask. "All right. Have it your way. I should have known you'd run scared. But if you ever have the guts to face what's between us, you know where to find me."

His body was rigid with suppressed emotion as he walked toward the door, and Halina expected him to slam out of her apartment. But he paused with his hand on the doorknob and asked without turning, "I don't suppose you'd care to hear the last installment about C.K.C.?"

Halina's eyes blurred with tears. He waited another moment, and when she didn't answer, he opened and closed the door with a soft click. Somehow the tiny sound had the ring of finality a full slam would not have had, and the tears rolled down her cheeks.

A WEEK LATER, as she was coming down from Randolph Que's apartment after her martial-arts lesson, Halina's carefully reconstructed world shattered. She had missed Cameron more than she'd thought possible. She had also been consumed by doubts and self-recrimination—but she had been reluctant to approach him for an explanation, afraid he might only confirm her suspicions.

Halina thought she had succeeded in piecing her life together, that her resolute plan to use work and sports once more as the panacea they'd proven to be in the past had worked out. But seeing Cameron opening the door for a beautiful older woman crumbled the flimsy defense she'd once again erected around herself.

Her cheeks, robbed of color at the sight of the elegant redhead, turned crimson as Cameron noticed her and his eyes ran expertly over her slightly thinner figure.

As his keen gaze took in her sudden rigidity and the unconscious accusation in her eyes, Halina saw sudden enlightenment in his face. Descending the last two steps through a great exertion of willpower, Halina stopped in the hall and nodded in greeting, forcing her voice into calmness.

"Hello, Cameron."

Proud of her steady tone, she was about to turn toward her apartment when Cameron's words stopped her. "Carol, this is Halina Barkley, my landlady." Unable to ignore the introduction, she came forward. "Halina, Carol Matthews, the lady you overheard me talking to last week."

153

"Oh, have you availed yourself of Cameron's marvelous talent, too?" The woman's Texas accent confused Halina as much as her friendly gesture of lacing her hand about Cameron's suit-clad arm. If Carol Matthews was intimately involved with him, would she be so obvious about it? Or inquire so blantantly about Halina's experience with Cameron?

Her confusion must have been mirrored in her eyes, because Cameron said with a bite to his voice that apparently went unnoticed by the redhead, "No. Halina is not aware of the last chapter in my life."

This time it was the woman who turned questioning eyes on Cameron. "What chapter is that, darling?"

Halina hurriedly interjected, "If you'll excuse me, I have a lot of things to attend to. I'm sure Cameron will explain his cryptic remark." Throwing Cameron a hostile glance, she added politely, "He's full of such priceless conversational gems."

Walking rapidly away, she called from the door to her apartment, "It was nice meeting you, Ms. Matthews."

"It's Mrs., dear."

"How nice for you." Halina smiled, unlocked the door, and hurriedly let herself in, in case Cameron had any ideas about detaining her longer.

Cameron's eyes had given off storm signals at her hurried departure, but at the moment Halina didn't want to deal with him. She felt suffocated by the maelstrom of passion he invoked in her. Ever since they'd met, he'd taken control of her thoughts and emotions to the point where she couldn't even concentrate properly on her lessons.

To add to her frustration, she was sorry now that she had not let Cameron tell her about what he'd termed the "last installment about C.K.C." Doubt, suppositions, and counterdenials would not be eating at her if she had.

After pacing the floor for several minutes, Halina told

herself she was being ridiculous and made herself sit down with a book. Reading had always proved a great relaxer before. But not even her favorite science fiction book, which she enjoyed rereading periodically, or the new historical novel she'd bought the day before, could hold her attention. She tried exercising next; when that failed also, she started cleaning.

Finally, unable to stand being inside the apartment any longer, she threw on slacks and a matching brown top; at the last minute she retraced her steps to get her Windbreaker from the hall closet. Autumn seemed to have arrived early this year, and it got quite cold and windy waiting on the platform of the el.

Her spur-of-the-moment decision to see Lorraine calmed her somewhat, as did the brisk walk to the station. Her friend had sounded delighted when she'd called, and Halina looked forward to their talk. Perhaps it would help to air her feelings, and Lorraine, despite her uncritical and adoring attitude toward the male gender, was a good listener.

Settled on a large artistic bean bag Lorraine had designed herself, Halina slowly sipped from her glass of wine. She felt more relaxed, having enjoyed her trip to Lincoln Avenue, where her friend owned a condominium in a very colorful block that boasted a Turkish bath on the corner.

Halina had always felt comfortable in her friend's living room. Its earth hues—all golds, reds, and greens— lifted her spirits and its warm coziness radiated welcoming acceptance. The apartment truly reflected the personality of its owner.

"I don't really see what your problem is," Lorraine was saying, her petite figure contorted in a yoga position on the floor. "According to you, this man is a terrific lover. And I say, more power to you. Do you know how rare it is to find a man nowadays who's sensitive to a woman's needs?"

"I don't see you pining away," Halina said dryly, looking at her friend's lustrous dark hair and intelligent brown eyes with warm affection. "Nothing seems to throw you."

"I've had my share of problems," Lorraine retorted, "but I think I'd love to have yours." Halina smiled at her friend's irrepressible humor and Lorraine added softly, "Besides, you're forgetting that there is a basic difference between you and me. I have a support group. Oh, I consider them more of a nuisance than anything else sometimes, and you've heard me complain about them often enough—parents who haven't realized I've been living on my own for six years now; older brothers who regularly check up on me; a grandmother who shows up unannounced to inspect the premises. . . ." Twisting her slender body into another position and rearranging the folds of her red hostess pajamas, Lorraine continued softly, "But I know they're always there. So I've been lucky, because no matter how independent a person is, she still needs someone. And you've been alone most of your life."

"That's a familiar pitch," Halina told her with amusement. "But I don't really need someone—if by someone you mean a man. I've gotten along without one all this time. Besides, why add complications to your life, especially when they can only bring pain?"

"I don't see how this guy can bring you any pain, though," Lorraine said in a puzzled tone. "You just told me he was a considerate lover."

"Those were not my exact words, but yes, I guess that's a fair way to describe Cameron," Halina said.

"Then what do you care if he's got a hundred other women? Or if he's a gigolo?" Lorraine asked with surprising denseness. "If the relationship is only physical,

I'd say you have a great thing going." Brushing her bangs out of her eyes, Lorraine added enthusiastically, "Just think of the experience the man brings into a relationship. What a terrific way to pick up a few pointers."

Halina got up with a groan of disgust at her friend's outrageous comment.

"You know me better than that, Lorraine," Halina said, exasperated by her friend's determined blindness. "I could never be seriously involved with a man who sleeps for a living." Her own words brought back Cameron's statement about his doing his best work at night. Could Cameron really have changed that much since the accident? She put her hands on her aching head; she just could not accept that Cameron would be that hedonistic.

"Even if Cameron is a gigolo, as you suspect, it's obvious he doesn't see you or treat you like those other women," Lorraine told her. "And really, why should you care one way or the other? You've already told me a couple of times that you're positive it's not love you feel for him."

"I don't need a commitment from Cameron," Halina began impatiently, and broke off as she realized that this was no longer true. It probably had never been true— but she'd been so busy looking back she'd overlooked the future, and the natural outcome of her developing relationship with him.

"You were saying?" Lorraine prodded her innocently.

Halina smiled grimly. "I have to hand it to you, Lorraine. You're good. You should've been a sleuth."

"This one was easy," Lorraine told her smugly. "No one carrying on and suffering as you are could be feeling only gratitude—or lust."

Uncoiling from her position, Lorraine went to the side table to refill their glasses. As she handed Halina hers, Lorraine told her in mild reproof, "You should have come to Mama Lorraine sooner." Although she was only a year older than Halina, she had always behaved maternally.

"And face having to put up with blind dates and constant invitations from you or the rest of the Morellis for parties, picnics, et cetera? No, thanks," she said forcefully, masking her emotion.

"I guess I won't have to worry about setting up any more blind dates, though," Lorraine said slyly, taking a sip of the cool wine.

"You never should have in the first place," Halina told her feelingly. "But there's nothing definite. I may have finally been forced into recognizing what's been driving me mad. But there's still Cameron to consider. And there's still a lot I don't know about him."

"I'd say you know the most important thing," Lorraine insisted.

Halina rubbed her forehead wearily. "I don't know, Lorraine. There has to be some answer to this puzzle. But I've been so busy resisting his attraction, and then, when he managed to breach my defenses, I tried so hard to delude myself it was a mere infatuation, that I haven't been thinking straight. I've probably jumped to the most insane conclusion."

"Since you've always been one of the most rational people I know, he's probably given you good cause," she said loyally. "It doesn't help that he's never told you what he does for a living now."

Halina drank some wine, trying to drown the bitter taste in her throat. "He tried to—once. I wouldn't let him."

"Well, you still can," Lorraine told her bracingly, coming to stand by her and putting an arm around her shoulders. "It's obvious the man cares for you. Maybe you could persuade him to change—if your suspicions turn out to be correct."

Halina gave her friend a strong hug and said huskily, "Thanks for listening, Lorraine." She put her glass down and, looking at the hand-painted clock on the living room wall, added guiltily, "And I'm sorry I've kept you up so late. I know you like to get to the boutique early in the morning."

"Anytime, and don't worry about the hour. Being the manager helps—I can come in late once in a while. Besides, I won't have to worry about keeping awake while I fight rush hour traffic. I've been trying car pooling this past month, and this week is my turn to rest while some other poor driver fights Michigan Avenue."

Halina picked up her Windbreaker from a nearby chair and hugged her friend good-bye.

"Good luck. And keep me posted," Lorraine requested as she saw Halina to the door.

"I will."

As Halina began walking down the stairs to the second floor, Lorraine called after her in a loud whisper, "Don't forget to put in a good word with your Don Juan—in case he has any nice friends."

Halina stared thoughtfully out the window as she rode on the Howard el, picturing the rooftops and trees covered in snow. Winter in Chicago was approaching, yet all of a sudden Halina could not conjure her usual enthusiasm for the round of Christmas parties, or even her yearly skiing trip.

She'd been reasonably content with her life and had rarely felt emptiness until she got to know Cam—as she'd begun to think of him. He had filled her life and thoughts with such vibrancy and color that she had naturally resisted him, sensing that if she let him become too important, it would be hard to fill the void when he left. The more he'd become woven into the fiber of her life, the more she'd denied it. But despite the determination that had served her well in the past, Cameron had successfully penetrated her shield.

Even when they had made love, Halina had tried to control and confine her emotions by labeling them "infatuation" and "physical attraction." Her lack of appetite the past few days had been a signal that she could no longer refuse to recognize her love—but still Halina had been afraid to do so.

She knew Cam no longer left for work in the mornings, wearing his three-piece suits, the epitome of the successful businessman. He'd told her that he was finishing his business shortly, and apparently he had. Perhaps if she hadn't been so confused and scared last week, she could have listened to Cam's explanation.

But she had tried to delude herself till the last minute. Her protective screen had been in place, an automatic habit of the past she'd been loath to shed. And now she was suffering the uncertainty and agony of love, laying herself open and vulnerable—but at least she was facing and dealing with her feelings.

Before she could approach Cam with her newly recognized knowledge, though, she needed some answers. Her instinct as a woman who loved told her that Cameron cared for her. How deeply, she still had to find out. And until all the doubts were resolved between them, Cameron would not know of her feelings.

Halina jogged the short distance to Barkley Court, loving the feel of the cool air on her cheeks. She breathed in deeply as she entered the courtyard at a slower pace.

She dug in her bag for her key as she walked toward the entrance to the building, and her heart almost stopped as a large figure detached itself from the shadows of an evergreen.

Halina's hands clutched her purse instinctively as a weapon, and she balanced her body automatically into a defensive position.

"Relax," a familiar voice drawled before the figure stepped into the pool of light. "No need to attack."

As she felt a surge of relief and her body began losing the tense crouch she'd adopted, it stiffened again at his next words.

"Where the hell have you been? It's almost three in the morning."

ALL THE WARM emotions Halina had felt as she'd savored the bittersweet experience of being in love fled before his male aggressiveness. What right did Cameron have to talk that way, demanding explanations? She had a right to a few of her own!

Halina walked around him, refusing to dignify his rude greeting with a response. But Cameron caught up with her at the door and pushed her against it. Halina opened her mouth to protest his violent action, but closed it as she felt his encircling arms cushioning her body against the thick glass.

"Yes, you'd do well to shut up!" Cameron bit out. Halina kept silent—not out of obedience, a reaction she was unfamiliar with, but because she was shocked at his loss of control. "I've been waiting for you for hours, and you show up jogging unconcernedly down the street at this hour. Jogging!" he repeated, disgust and disbelief mirrored in equal measure in his pale face.

"You seem to be fixated on the hour," Halina said calmly, attempting to remove his arms from around her body. His iron grip tightened even more. "And what do you have against jogging?"

"I have nothing against jogging," he said through gritted teeth, his body coiled as if to strike. Halina stared up at him patiently, waiting for a chance to make her move. "What I object to is not knowing where you are, finding your car in the parking lot, and then seeing you running home like a wood nymph."

163

She rather liked his comparison, but didn't think it was the time to thank him for the compliment. She doubted he'd meant it as such. Instead, she said flippantly, "The parking lot is the usual location for a car." At his murderous look, she added prudently, "I decided to take the el to my friend's place."

"At this hour? What kind of friend would let you come back on the train so late?"

Accustomed to taking care of herself, which included riding the train at odd hours sometimes, Halina felt she'd had enough. "None of your business," she responded to his fierce whisper. Since he hadn't made much of an effort to see her the past few days, his concern was a bit out of place. "If you don't mind, I'd like to go to bed. I've had a long day, and I . . ."

"But I do mind," Cameron said silkily, pushing the door open and forcing her inside. "This is the second time you've done this to me, sweetheart. I don't relish going crazy over your safety. I have to leave in a few hours, but we'll take care of some things tonight before I leave."

His mouth began a deliberate descent toward hers, and Halina moved her head sideways to avoid it, his last words ringing in her mind. "You're leaving?"

His answer was mumbled against the slender curve of her neck. "I have to take care of an emergency in Texas and finalize certain transactions. I should be back in two to three weeks."

Halina wanted more information and made the mistake of turning her head to see his expression. Cameron swooped down on her parted mouth with the speed of a predator, and her words remained unsaid.

As his lips plundered hers with savage intent, his hands unsnapped the buttons on her Windbreaker and roamed her body with rough intimacy. But the anger, worry, and frustration she perceived in him seemed to be ebbing. Halina sensed Cameron's battle with himself, one part of him wanting to punish her for the pain she'd somehow caused him yet a stronger part instinctively tempering his caresses, subduing their harshness into explosive passion.

Halina fell victim to his sensual expertise as Cameron pressed her against the wall, molding her curves to his desire-hardened frame. Her own hands reached for the thick black hair curling into his sweater, and her fingers delighted in the rough, velvety feel.

But she recovered her senses, clamping down on the fiery arrows of need shooting through her as Cameron cupped one swollen mound in his hand, rolling the nipple lazily between thumb and forefinger, and grasped her back to bring her closer to the pulsing vibrancy of his body, murmuring thickly, "Let's go to bed."

The incinerating flames of rage freed her mind from the numbing fumes of passion, and Halina sliced him with the edge of her palm squarely in the solar plexus, experiencing no remorse as the air left his lungs. Stiffening her surrender-softened body, Halina pushed away from Cameron as he was trying to recover his breath. After hurriedly unlocking the door, she ran in on trembling limbs.

"Hello, Halina?"

Halina dropped the dust cloth and sat down on the couch, her stomach somersaulting at Cameron's voice. She kept her own even and friendly as she answered his greeting.

"I'm planning on coming back tomorrow—though I'm not sure what time I'll be getting away."

"Have you finished all your business in Texas, then?" she asked, torturing the hem of her skirt as she waited nervously for his answer.

"All loose ends tied up," he told her in a satisfied tone. "My old career is finally behind me. Now I can concentrate fully on the new one."

"And do you think your new career will be as satisfying?" she asked cautiously.

"More so. I think it will definitely be more rewarding."

Halina liked the happy lilt in his voice, but she was unsure what it meant. Taking a deep breath, she told him casually, "I'd like to hear about this latest chapter in your life." Throwing caution to the winds, she added, "If you still want to tell me about it."

The pause that ensued stretched her nerves to the breaking point, and then she heard Cameron say huskily, "Thought you'd never ask."

There were raised voices in the background and Cameron said hurriedly, "Halina, I've got to go. I'm in the middle of a conference, but I wanted to let you know when I was coming back. I'll tell you the latest C.K.C. installment when I return."

"I'll be waiting," she told him softly, and held on to the phone long after the line went dead.

Rousing herself from her musings, Halina continued dusting, telling herself she'd better keep busy or the next twenty-four hours would never go by.

After the way they'd parted Halina hadn't expected Cameron to phone. But he had, twice including this call, surprising her yet again. The first time had been a brief call on the day of his arrival, and Cameron had apologized for his behavior—after telling her wryly that she had to perfect her hit; he was still alive. Halina had apologized also, but Cameron had waved aside her comment that she usually did not go around hitting people by telling her he'd had it coming.

His first call had stirred the embers of hope within her; his second had fanned them to life. And Halina found it excruciating waiting for Cameron to come back in order to straighten out all misunderstandings.

* * *

Halina taught a class the next morning, and then had a tutoring session with a student who could not grasp any concepts of science. After an hour of steady and patient repetition, the boy began to show some signs of understanding, and Halina felt exhausted but happy with the beginning results.

Tense with anticipation, she called from the college to see if Cameron was in, and then again from home after taking a quick shower. When Cameron didn't answer, Halina decided to use her passkey and wait for him at his apartment. She was too anxious to see him and resolve their misunderstandings to call every few minutes until he arrived. Slipping into black pants and a pearl-gray sweater, Halina was about to leave when Mrs. Tate knocked on her door.

Ordinarily she would have spent a half hour chatting with the delightful lady, but fortunately Mrs. Tate was leaving for her bridge club date and stayed only long enough to pay her rent and get a receipt.

Halina quickly left her own apartment and hurried down the hall. As she let herself into Cameron's, she knew he'd already arrived. She could hear muted voices and laughter—and one voice was definitely a woman's. About to withdraw from the room and retreat as she'd done once before, Halina stopped. She squared her shoulders and walked across the living room with fierce determination. A cold film of perspiration covered her body as she approached the smaller bedroom, but she forced herself to go on.

A gasp escaped her lips as she saw the same blonde who'd left Cameron's apartment the night they'd gone dancing. She was sitting just inside the room—and she was nude. Gritting her teeth, Halina advanced a few more steps, only to halt as Cameron came out of that room, jeans hanging low on his hips, yellow shirt open halfway down his chest.

His hair was tousled, covering one side of his forehead, his flesh smooth and deeply tanned. Halina noticed with clinical detachment that his scar was no longer red but was healing very well. Her attention was drawn back to his face as he recovered from his surprise and asked her, "How did you get in here? I tried calling you from the airport, and again when I got home, but got no answer."

He walked up to her to take her in his arms and kiss her, but Halina evaded his mouth so that his kiss dropped on her cheek. "The door was open, and you couldn't reach me because I was at the college."

His brows rose at her expressionless tone and he asked, "Anything wrong?"

Halina gave him a wan smile and said, "Of course not. What could possibly be wrong?" Then, deciding that diplomacy would serve no useful purpose and that she might as well resolve the situation now, she told him, "It seems you have company. Am I disturbing you?"

"In many ways," he said, grinning suggestively, "but not in the way you're implying. The company you're referring to is a client."

Halina paled at his words, but he didn't seem to notice as he draped an arm around her shoulders and said, "Come on, I'll introduce you." Cupping her chin with the hand resting on her shoulder, he raised her face to his and told her huskily, "You must have figured out what I do for a living already, but I'll fill you in on all the details tonight, after I finish with Bea."

She looked at him mutely and then lowered her eyes, trying to concentrate on her legs, which felt wooden, the steps she was taking seemingly engulfed in quicksand. Cameron let her go in first and followed close behind. When Halina stopped at the entrance, he turned questioningly to her.

Halina felt her earlier lethargy multiply tenfold. She was incapable of movement as she saw a canvas—faithfully replicating the beautiful nude figure of the blonde, out of sight at the moment.

As she turned to look for the woman, Cameron noticed her expression and asked, "What's the matter, Halina?"

Halina managed a sickly smile and answered, "Well, I guess I'm just a bit surprised." The understatement of the year! "I was not expecting..." Here she faltered, but Cameron was quick to jump in.

"Just *what* were you expecting?"

"Well, I guess I never pictured you as an artist."

"Of course I'm an artist. I thought you knew, when I told you I wanted to introduce you." A puzzled frown brought his thick eyebrows together and he asked, "Why else would I have all these women here?"

Then, as her expression told him what Halina had obviously thought was his business, his frown smoothed and he began chuckling. A moment later he was roaring, and Halina felt like kicking him—especially when a feminine voice piped up behind her, "What's so funny, Cameron?"

Halina turned and saw the blonde coming from behind a partition in the far corner of the room. Now a caftan covered her luscious full figure.

The woman approached Halina and extended her hand, introducing herself with easy grace, "I'm Bea Johnson. I was just putting on a little something to ward off the chill. This boy is a slave driver." Looking at Halina closely, Bea Johnson added delightedly, "And you must be Halina Barkley."

Halina blinked and answered, "Yes—yes, I am. But how..." she began, casting a surprised look at Cameron, who stood silently and laughingly devouring her with his eyes, his thumbs hooked in his jeans.

"Cameron described you perfectly to my husband and me on the plane." At Halina's blank look, she explained, "We decided to fly in with Cameron at the last minute." Halina still felt lost and wanted to insert a question, but

Bea was already continuing, "I'm glad Cameron has finally made the right decision—even if his father's not too happy about it. I always felt it was a shame to let his talent go to waste."

"Oh, Cameron's talented, all right," Halina agreed softly, slowly beginning to regain her scattered wits.

Bea smiled charmingly and Cameron inclined his head in mocking acceptance. "Well, he told us he'd only be doing a few portraits, and I convinced him to paint mine." She perched on a stool a few feet away from the canvas and told Halina conversationally, "You see, Cameron had done a life-size portrait of my teen-age daughter." At Halina's raised brows, Bea laughed. "Clothed. Although Tildy was hoping for a different version. And then that got me to thinking that Jared would be thrilled to have a nude painting of me in our bedroom."

"I see," Halina said, but her tone was not very convincing.

Bea's blue eyes widened. "You mean you didn't know about Cameron's painting until just now?"

"No," Halina answered succinctly. Smiling sweetly at Cameron, she said, "It seems there's a lot Cameron conveniently left out."

"I wanted to see if I could succeed first. That's why I took a few months' semisabbatical." Cameron entered the conversation for the first time, answering Bea but looking at Halina. She looked back with a decided lack of warmth.

"I see." This time the two words were loaded with meaning.

"But surely you didn't think that I—that Cameron and I—" Bea broke into peals of laughter, but Halina could tell the woman was flattered. "After all, I'm thirteen years older than Cameron," she added when she'd regained her breath.

"Your face and figure would put a twenty year old to shame," Halina said dryly, and refrained from mentioning that she'd thought Cameron capable of being involved with a fair number of other clients.

"Why, thank you, darling," Bea said, obviously pleased. "Jared will be thrilled when I tell him about this small mix-up." A small quick frown puckered her smooth forehead and Bea mused aloud, "On second thought..."

"You husband might not be so delighted?" Halina supplied helpfully.

"Well, you know how men are!" Bea said dismissively.

Halina muttered, "Amen," and saw by the slight narrowing of the light-green eyes that Cam had heard her.

"But really, Cameron, you should have told Halina the truth. I know Carol and Georgia came up from Texas for portraits also, before you close up shop and begin concentrating on landscapes. This poor girl must have been worried sick."

"Oh, I wouldn't put it quite that strongly," Halina amended silkily.

"Neither would I," Cameron said dryly. "You have that turned around. She was making a wreck out of me."

"Well, you probably deserved it, then," Bea said severely. Turning to Halina, she added, "You see, the reason I wanted Cameron to do my portrait is because I trust him—and most important, my husband would trust him. And because I feel comfortable with Cameron. After all, I've known Cameron since he was in his teens, and we are great friends of the parents of this dear boy."

Cameron winced at the last two words, and Halina smiled with real enjoyment. Now that the enigma had been solved, all her fears and uncertainties had dissolved too...to be replaced by a slow-burning anger.

Knowing she had to get out before she exploded, Halina told herself Cam would have an evening to remember. "I came over to ask you to dinner," she informed Cameron in a cool, polite tone, "because there were several things I wanted to discuss with you."

"Will nine o'clock be too late?" Cameron asked as he resumed working. Indicating his hands and old work clothes, he said, "I'd like to take a shower and change before I come over."

"Nine will be fine," Halina said politely. Addressing Bea more warmly, she added, "And you're welcome also—and your husband—whenever you finish your sitting."

"Thank you, dear. But I'll have to be running as soon as Cameron puts on the finishing touches. Unfortunately, Jared insisted on accompanying me this trip out, and he's cooling his heels in the hotel while I finish my 'shopping.'" Resuming her seat, Bea said laughingly, "And will Jared be surprised when he realizes he's been suspicious and jealous for no reason."

"Well, then, I won't keep you," Halina said, beginning to back out of the room. She knew now why Cameron had kept the door closed the few times she'd been in his apartment. And why he'd had little time to furnish it.

"I hope you're not upset, my dear. You see, we don't mind having to seek him out in his retreat," Bea was saying, "but it does rather limit our time with him, having our portraits painted long distance, so to speak," she accused Cameron with a charming pout.

"I understand," Halina said. "It's been a pleasure meeting you."

"Likewise, my dear. Please make sure to come over when Cameron comes back to Texas for visits."

Halina made a suitably polite response, refusing to commit herself. Whether she and Cameron went anywhere together remained to be seen.

Chapter
14

WHILE SHE PREPARED the roast and vegetables, Halina had time to simmer down. She realized that they had both been at fault: Cameron for not telling her of his painting and plans, and she for not trusting him or having the courage to ask him outright.

Therefore, by the time Cameron came over, she was no longer angry. But she was still upset enough to avoid making things easy for him.

She greeted him coolly as she opened the door, quickly stepping out of his reach when he went to take her in his arms. Leading the way into the dining room, Halina felt somewhat vindicated as Cameron stopped stock-still at its arched entrance, his eyes taking in the seduction scene: soft music, candlelight, and wine bottles—white for him, red for her—cooling amid crystal and silver.

Cameron turned slowly toward Halina, one black eyebrow shooting up in silent questioning. She ignored it for the moment and leaned over the table to get two crystal glasses.

"Some wine?"

"Something stronger, please," Cameron said with sardonic inflection. Taking off his tan sport jacket, he draped it over a velvet-upholstered dining chair and moved to her side. "I have a feeling I'm going to need it."

Halina smiled distantly and served him bourbon from a small wet bar in a corner of the dining room. She gave him the glass and poured red wine for herself.

173

"If you'll excuse me, I have to check on the roast."

From the frustrated look on Cameron's face, that was the last thing he wanted right now. But it was also obvious that he was willing to go along with her for the moment.

From then on, the evening progressed perfectly.

The meal was excellent: The meat was tender and juicy, the vegetables cooked to perfection. Cameron had two servings of her homemade Black Forest cake and was the correct gentleman throughout dinner.

Except for the occasional straying of his glance to the deep V neckline of her hot-pink jumpsuit, and the twitching of a muscle each time she leaned over or accidentally brushed against him with finely honed precision, Cameron remained outwardly calm.

Halina suggested taking coffee in the living room, and Cameron agreed readily. He offered to help her do the dishes, and when Halina said they could wait, he helped her clear the table. He carried their wineglasses into the living room, since the coffee wasn't ready, and waited until she sat on the couch before settling his long length next to her.

Halina noticed the subtle maneuver and silently applauded it. She marveled at his control, because hers had started to slip. She found it hard to keep her eyes from the tight-fitting black slacks and black shirt open at the neck, which revealed a smattering of dark hair. And her hands were itching to caress the male body sprawled with deceiving indolence next to her.

Shifting sideways, Halina leaned an elbow on the back of the couch so her neckline would become even more plunging, and felt the brass buttons straining. Noticing how his eyes were drawn there, she smiled innocently and asked, "How was your trip from Texas?"

"Damn it, Halina! You couldn't care less about my trip from Texas."

"All right," she conceded calmly. "What should we

talk about?" She took a sip of her wine and said with velvet softness, "About your artistic endeavors?"

His eyes narrowed as they took in her relaxed pose. "That's more like it," he said silkily. "You've always gone straight to the point. I'm just surprised that you're not more upset."

"Why should I be? You said you wanted to see if you were a success—although from what Bea disclosed, that was never in doubt. You certainly don't have to tell me your every move."

"We both know that's not true. I owed you an explanation—but the waiting game became important in itself as a way to have you around me. And let me tell you, sweetheart, you were not very approachable at first. I also had to see if I could cope with a less frenetic way of life. As I've told you, I came back to Chicago not only to see if I could paint, or make a living from it, but to get away from it all, to exercise my options."

"And I was just one of many options?" Halina asked, beginning to feel the stirrings of anger again.

"No, and you know it." He paused and added huskily, "There were a couple of buildings I'd considered staying in when I first came to Chicago. But as soon as I saw you, I was sold on Barkley Court."

"How convenient for you, to have me down the hall," Halina said mockingly.

"Halina." Cameron's voice warned her that she was pushing him.

She crossed her legs, her black sandals peeping from under the softly flared legs of her jumpsuit, and couldn't resist a little more teasing. "Actually, it turned out quite well for both of us. I can't deny your lovemaking was terrific—after the first time—and I've been thinking that since our physical chemistry is so fantastic, we should continue indefinitely." Noticing that Cameron's eyes fairly shot off green sparks, she added casually, "But I would want a certain condition, of course."

"And that is?" Cameron asked impassively, only the tiny pulse in his temple revealing his imminent loss of control.

"That I engage your exclusive services, so to speak."

"So to speak," he repeated with smooth irony. "I take it, then, that you wouldn't want any other women in my life?"

"Not for as long as our understanding lasts. It would be too impractical and tiresome to find naked women around every time I happened to come over. You understand, I'm sure."

"Oh, I understand," Cameron said with a dangerous smile. He opened the buttons of his shirt slowly, and just looking at those long-fingered hands made Halina weak with longing. "I understand that while I've been feeling guilty about not having told you about my painting, and worrying over having lost your trust, you've been taking your own sweet revenge."

His shirt was completely open now and Cameron leaned forward to take the glass from her hands and put both glasses on the end table next to her.

Suddenly nervous as the naked expanse of chest almost touched her, Halina coughed delicately to clear her arid throat.

"I don't know what you mean," she began, edging slightly away from him.

"I think you know exactly what I mean. Just as you know there's been nothing between those women and me." He paused, then added thoughtfully, "But weren't so sure a few weeks ago, right? That's why you froze me out, and then tore my guts apart with that accusing stare on the steps that day."

"You have to admit that things didn't look too good for you then," Halina said, trying to regain the momentum she'd lost. Or, rather, Cameron had stolen.

"I had hoped you would have trusted me."

His softly spoken words hit a raw nerve and Halina

reacted defensively. "Would you have trusted me implicitly?"

"Yes," was the prompt, sure response.

"That's probably because you knew of my past experiences," Halina said coolly.

"Do you think I was so sure of you that I thought you'd fallen madly in love with me on the basis of one night? When you'd fought me at every turn, and even told me we shouldn't see each other again?"

When Halina stared at him in stony silence, Cameron swore softly under his breath. Then, pressing her down on the couch, he covered her body with his.

"You must have seen Georgia in the apartment, right?" he asked gently, his fingers tracing the line of her brow and nose with bone-melting tenderness.

"Was that a blonde, redhead, or brunette?" Halina asked with dry sarcasm.

Cameron groaned and said huskily, "Brunette. And I see why you're so angry at me. I never stopped to think what you'd make of their comings and goings. I guess, if I'd considered it, I still would have thought you'd come to me and demand an explanation."

"I might have, if it hadn't been for my scars from Jeff." Then, realizing that she was thawing too quickly, she added firmly, "And I'm not angry at you." It was true now. All her anger had dissipated in the face of his revelations. She found herself responding to the warm hard weight of Cameron's body with all the passion and love in her being. But Cameron had not told her yet how he really felt about her. She knew that he must love her, but she needed to hear him say the words.

Cameron covered her mouth with his, as if to silence her into submission. He nibbled on her lips time and time again, leaving them tender and sensitive, and his hands went to her sash, untying it.

Halina remained relaxed but unresponsive under his mouth and hands, calling on every ounce of reserve. At last Cameron raised his head, his eyes dark with arousal.

"Punishing me?" he asked thickly, sexual tension too long repressed evident in the rigidity of his legs entwined with hers.

Halina's eyes widened, their silvery depths innocent. "I don't know what you mean. Do you feel you deserve punishment?"

"I'll show you what I mean," he growled, his mouth swooping down to claim her lips once more with heady mastery. This time she allowed her tongue to play with his, but when Cameron began opening the jumpsuit's buttons, which ran all the way to her navel, Halina grabbed his wrists.

With obvious effort Cameron refocused his glazed eyes on hers and murmured with amusement, "I'd forgotten how stubborn you can be. And I am not in the mood or the condition to wrestle with you at the moment."

The delicate arching of her brow widened his smile, and he rolled away from her to lie comfortably on his side, one leg draped possessively over her thighs, his hands holding her wrists in a firm but gentle grasp.

Halina tested his grip, trying to uncuff her hands, but his hold, while still gentle, closed like iron manacles. Her reddened lips curved into a mocking grin, which he returned, saying, "Purely self-defense. You pack a mean punch in more ways than one, sweetheart."

"What if I promise not to inflict any serious damage?"

He considered her silently for a minute, his smoldering gaze taking in the sparkle of her gray eyes and the peachy softness of her cheeks, and zeroing in on the tip of a pink tongue, which wet the full lips in a deliberately provocative motion.

He sighed and unshackled her wrists slowly, his eyes narrowing as she stretched her arms before lowering them again, the soft, billowy sleeves brushing against his chest on the way down.

"All right. What do you want from me?"

Halina raised herself on one elbow and looked down at the strong, slightly flushed handsome face, resisting the urge to follow its chiseled contours with her fingers. "It seems to me, Cameron Connors, that you're the one who wants something. And like the typical male, only just one thing."

His tightly leashed control snapping, he pulled her roughly on top of him, drawing a deep breath when the warm cushion of her breasts rested against his chest. "You're wrong. I don't want just one thing, I want everything—your body, your soul, your mind, your heart."

His eyes burned into hers and Halina quivered from the deep emotion reflected there.

"And when did you come to such a decision?" Halina whispered, all anger and hurt and past fears washed away by his love.

"I decided I wanted your body the moment I saw you that first day, and the rest the first time I made love to you and you became a part of me."

The last of Halina's resistance melted away and she gave in to her overriding impulse to run her fingers from his jaw past his cheekbone into his hair, luxuriating in the feel of the straight springy mass.

"I always knew you were a wolf, Cam Connors," Halina said with a soft sigh as her hands fluttered to rest on his shoulders.

He tensed. "What did you call me?"

"Cameron Connors," she said with mischief shining in her eyes.

He embraced her punishingly, his kisses a potent drug that robbed her of breath and reason, and then demanded once more, "What did you call me?"

Halina whispered the syllable, tasting the sweet sound on her trobbing lips.

"Cam."

Cameron undressed both of them quickly, his hands

caressing her body as he removed her clothes with maddening efficiency. As he nibbled on the round curve of her shoulder, his body fitting hers intimately, his voice vibrated his need with petal-softness on her skin. "God, it's been so long."

Halina turned her head into the brown column of his neck and answered unsteadily, "It's only been a few weeks."

"Forever," he murmured, his hands tracing an erotic pattern against the soft ivory skin of her stomach. Sensing her mounting need, he wove his shudder-inducing strokes lower, along the silken length of her inner thighs, and then toward the very center of her desire, threatening to consume her with his gentle, knowing touch.

Halina imitated his movements, wanting to know him, feeling the liquid fires of love and passion flow over her as she gave herself fully to his embrace.

She caressed his sun-browned skin, which rippled under her butterfly-soft touch, and then he was guiding her and a groan erupted from the very depths of him as her hands found his straining manhood. Time ceased to exist as Halina rejoiced in the fact that she was able to elicit such a stormy, passionate response from him.

Cameron kissed her, a hard, brief kiss that spoke of his love. Rising from the couch, he picked her up with reverent care.

Lying down on the thick carpeting, Cameron lowered Halina on top of him and began an all-consuming attack on her senses until she was grabbing weakly at his shoulders.

"Please, Cam," she whispered.

Cameron rolled her onto her back and covered her body with his. "God, how I love you, sweetheart," he pledged huskily as he joined them with an urgency that fully matched her own wild need....

* * *

As they stood atop the Sears Tower two days later, the city at their feet like a glittering diadem below the 110-story building, Cameron pressed her body closer into the hard curve of his.

"I liked sleeping in your bed last night—now that I know how to turn without falling off," Halina told Cameron softly, liking the sound of his answering chuckle as it vibrated from his chest into her back. "Don't you think we should bring your bed over as soon as possible?"

"Until we remodel completely, we could always take turns," Cameron suggested, amused.

"Remodeling will take a while," Halina said, happily envisioning the time when their two apartments would be joined, so that one would provide living space and the other a studio for Cameron, and an office for her.

"We've got all the time in the world," he whispered against her ear, sending shivers skipping along her nerve endings.

"Will you mind not working on nude paintings after you finish Bea's?"

"But I won't totally, remember?" Cameron answered throatily. "I'll have a full-time permanent model, who I expect to pose for me regularly."

Turning in the circle of his arms, Halina told him, "I guess I'm worried that you'll find painting too sedate. You might miss all the excitement and daily judgments that went with the type of position you had, and your father won't be too pleased with your decision."

"That is one of the reasons I came to Chicago in the first place and opened up a temporary branch here. I needed to make a choice away from the hustle and bustle of all the companies in Texas, and also away from my father's area of influence. He can be quite persuasive."

"I just hope you don't regret your decision later on." Halina told him, caressing his cheek and trailing one finger across the firm line of his mouth. "I don't care what job you have as long as you're happy. If you thrive on challenge . . ."

"I have all the challenge I need right here," he told her, taking a nip of the finger outlining his lips. "The electronics firm had always been my father's dream, not mine. I guess I would have realized it sooner or later. The accident was just a catalyst."

Opening her coat, he slipped his hands inside and rested them on her waist, rubbing the wool of her sweater dress against her skin. "You—and keeping you happy—are all the excitement and challenge I need," he told her huskily. "And while painting may be more sedate than engaging in takeovers, or dealing with acquisitions, I also find it more personally rewarding. Besides," he added, "I won't give up business altogether. I'll still troubleshoot two or three times a year, especially at first, to augment our income. But free-lancing will allow me to set my own time and hours."

Raising an arm to thread his fingers through her unbound chestnut hair, he asked, "Question is, will you be able to put up with a struggling painter?"

"Better than a successful gigolo," she whispered. "I'd like to keep your talents in the family."

He chuckled. "For that, lady, the going price is marriage. How about next week?"

Forgetting the crowd of tourists admiring the view from the intimate gloom of the observation tower, Halina encircled his neck and brought the dark head down to hers for an answer.

WATCH FOR
6 NEW TITLES EVERY MONTH!

Second Chance at Love

All of the above titles are $1.75 per copy except where noted

WHAT READERS SAY ABOUT
SECOND CHANCE AT LOVE BOOKS

"Your books are the greatest!"
—*M. N., Carteret, New Jersey**

"I have been reading romance novels for quite some time, but the SECOND CHANCE AT LOVE books are the most enjoyable."
—*P. R., Vicksburg, Mississippi**

"I enjoy SECOND CHANCE [AT LOVE] more than any books that I have read and I do read a lot."
—*J. R., Gretna, Louisiana**

"I really think your books are exceptional...I read Harlequin and Silhouette and although I still like them, I'll buy your books over theirs. SECOND CHANCE [AT LOVE] is more interesting and holds your attention and imagination with a better story line..."
—*J. W., Flagstaff, Arizona**

"I've read many romances, but yours take the 'cake'!"
—*D. H., Bloomsburg, Pennsylvania**

"Have waited ten years for *good* romance books. Now I have them."
—*M. P., Jacksonville, Florida**

*Names and addresses available upon request